HACK/SLASH™
RESURRECTION

VOLUME 2
BLOOD SIMPLE

A TIM SEELEY / STEFANO CASELLI PRODUCTION

Written by **TINI HOWARD**

Art by **CELOR**

Colors by **K. MICHAEL RUSSELL**

Lettering by **CRANK!**

Production by **RYAN BREWER**

Edits by **TIM SEELEY**

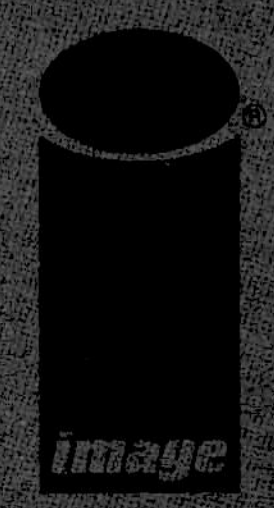

IMAGE COMICS, INC.

IMAGECOMICS.COM

HACK/SLASH: RESURRECTION, VOL. 2: BLOOD SIMPLE. First printing. December 2018. Published by Image Comics, Inc. Office of publication: 2701 NW Vaughn St., Suite 780, Portland, OR 97210.
ISBN: 978-1-5343-0879-4.

ISSUE 7 COVER BY
TIM SEELEY & K. MICHAEL RUSSELL

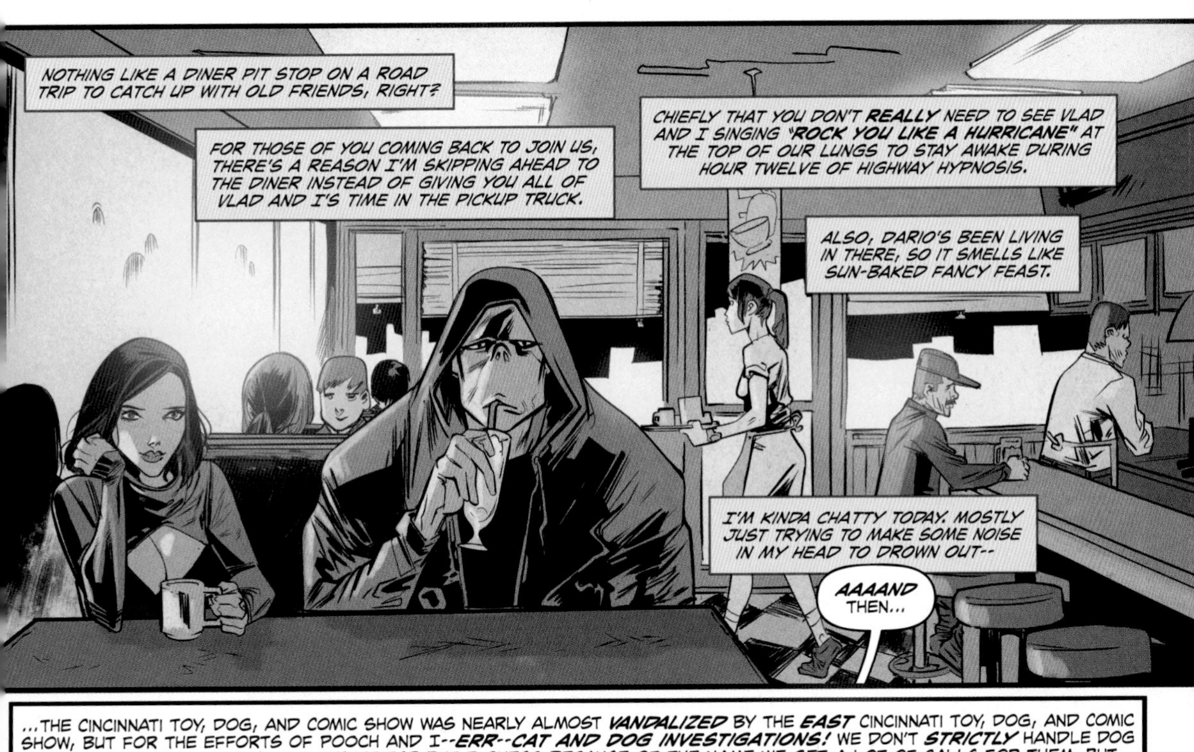
NOTHING LIKE A DINER PIT STOP ON A ROAD TRIP TO CATCH UP WITH OLD FRIENDS, RIGHT?
FOR THOSE OF YOU COMING BACK TO JOIN US, THERE'S A REASON I'M SKIPPING AHEAD TO THE DINER INSTEAD OF GIVING YOU ALL OF VLAD AND I'S TIME IN THE PICKUP TRUCK.
CHIEFLY THAT YOU DON'T **REALLY** NEED TO SEE VLAD AND I SINGING **"ROCK YOU LIKE A HURRICANE"** AT THE TOP OF OUR LUNGS TO STAY AWAKE DURING HOUR TWELVE OF HIGHWAY HYPNOSIS.
ALSO, DARIO'S BEEN LIVING IN THERE, SO IT SMELLS LIKE SUN-BAKED FANCY FEAST.
I'M KINDA CHATTY TODAY. MOSTLY JUST TRYING TO MAKE SOME NOISE IN MY HEAD TO DROWN OUT--
AAAAND THEN...

...THE CINCINNATI TOY, DOG, AND COMIC SHOW WAS NEARLY ALMOST ***VANDALIZED*** BY THE ***EAST*** CINCINNATI TOY, DOG, AND COMIC SHOW, BUT FOR THE EFFORTS OF POOCH AND I--***ERR--CAT AND DOG INVESTIGATIONS!*** WE DON'T ***STRICTLY*** HANDLE DOG AND CAT RELATED CRIMES AND MYSTERIES? BUT I GUESS BECAUSE OF THE NAME WE GET A LOT OF CALLS FOR THEM. BUT, OH BOY, VANDALS? AT THE TOY, DOG, AND COMIC SHOW? POOCHIE AND I PUT A STOP TO ***THAT!***

THE ***WINNING*** DOG WAS A ***BORZOI*** NAMED ***SAVAGE DRAG--***
CAT--

BURGER, BURGER, FLAPJACKS, AND TWO DOUBLE BURGERS, RARE, NO BUN.
YUM!!
POOCHIE'S FEAST OF FILTHMEATS!

I'VE BEEN IN THE TRUCK FOR ***TWELVE HOURS***, SO I'M GONNA PUT THIS WHOLE BURGER IN MY MOUTH WHILE YOU EXPLAIN WHAT YOU NEED VLAD AND I'S HELP WITH, OKAY?
STAY ON TOPIC.

RIGHT! SO--

"WE GOT A CALL LAST WEEK FROM THIS COUPLE..."
--AND WITH THE POSTAL WORKER IMPLICATED AS THE DRIVING FORCE BEHIND THE SCENE, DETECTIVE CAT CURIO ALLOWED HERSELF A KISS ON THE CHEEK FROM EACH OF THE RESCUED GO-GO BOYS BEFORE GETTING BACK TO WORK.
BZZZT BZZZT
YESSSS... YESSS... PETTINGS... GIVE PETTINGS TO MEEE...

CAT AND DOG INVESTIGATIONS, THIS IS DETECTIVE CAT CURIO SPEAKING, HOW MAY I DIRECT YOUR CALL?
MISS... CURIO. THANK YOU. THIS IS ELAINE BURROUGHS--
ONE MOMENT.

I'M SO SORRY, I'M HAVING ONE OF MY VISIONS. HOW INCONVENIENT.
CAN I PUT YOU ON WITH MY HUSBAND INSTEAD?

CAT. THIS IS TROY BURROUGHS. HOW CAN I HELP YOU?
YES... LET ME LOVE... LET POOCH TASTE YOU...
WELL, SIR, YOUR WIFE...
SHE'S REALLY SOMETHING, ISN'T SHE?
SIR, IT'S THAT YOU CALLED ME...

SO YOU DID!
LISTEN, PEACHCAKE, MY WIFE AND I--YOU'VE PROBABLY HEARD OF US--ARE FANS OF YOUR LITTLE OPERATION THERE.
HEARD OF--
IF YOU HAVEN'T HEARD OF US, JUST DO A LITTLE GOOGLE. I'LL WAIT.
YOU GOOGLING?
AH, I'LL JUST TELL YOU. ELAINE AND I ARE THE PREMIER PARANORMAL INVESTIGATORS, DEMONOLOGISTS, AND THE ONLY MARRIED GHOST HUNTERS IN THE TRI-COUNTY AREA.
JAMES DEAN?
IS THAT YOU AGAIN?
I'M A MARRIED WOMAN...
WE'VE JUST GOTTEN A CONTRACT TO LOOK INTO THE OLD DEMARCO PLACE, BUT WE CAN'T SEEM TO AGREE ON WHO GETS TO HOLD THE CAMERA AND WHO GETS TO TALK TO IT.
WE NEED ANOTHER SET OF HANDS--ONE THAT ISN'T SQUEAMISH WHEN IT COMES TO THE PARANORMAL.
ARE YOU IN, JELLYBEAN?

UHHH...
PERFECT.
SEE YOU THURSDAY, 7PM.
BRING HORS D'OEUVRES!
CLIK

I SEE...
WELL, YOU DID THE RIGHT THING BY CALLING US.
WAP
THANK YOU!
I JUST HAVE A BAD FEELING ABOUT THIS, AND I DON'T WANT TO NOT GO?
OF COURSE WE'RE GOING. IT'S CREEPY, AND POSSIBLY DANGEROUS.
"THAT'S LIKE THE ONLY THING WE HAVE IN COMMON."
WE'RE HERE.
HI, MR. AND MRS. BURROUGHS?
I'M CAT, AND I'VE BROUGHT MY FRIENDS AND CONSULTANTS, VLAD AND CASSIE HACK--
HURK!

ENCHANTÉ, MISS HACK.
LEGGO--

MY MISTAKE!
I DIDN'T REALIZE YOUR HUSBAND WAS HERE WITH YOU!

YOUR WIFE IS A VISION--
HE'S NOT MY HUSBAND, AND HE'S NOT THE ONE WHO TOLD YOU TO NOT TOUCH ME.
I DID THAT.
DARLING?

MY LOVE!
SO THRILLED YOU'VE CONVALESCED. I KNOW YOUR LAST SPIRITUAL CONGRESS WITH RASPUTIN REALLY TOOK IT OUT OF YOU.
THANK YOU MY DARLING.
I SENSED OUR GUEST HAD ARRIVED?
YOU SENSED THAT WE KNOCKED ON THE DOOR.

INDEED, AND SHE EVEN BROUGHT CONSULTANTS!
PRO BONO CONSULTANTS, I'M ASSUMING, SINCE WE WEREN'T ASKED ABOUT HIRING THEM!
CAT...

EXCELLENT.
LET'S BEGIN.

WHERE'S YOUR DOG? HE WAS HOLDING THE SPOTLIGHT, AND YOUR BIG FRIEND WAS DOING *SOUND*...

CAT?

OOOUAAAUUUGH!!

SHE'S AN ANGRY SPIRIT!
NO SHIT!
TROY, THE SACRIMETER!
CAT, ARE YOU GETTING THIS?!

UH HUH! I STILL COULD USE MORE LIGHT, THOUGH.
POOOOCH, WHERE ARE YOU?!

AUOOOWOOOUUUUUGH--
IN NOMINE PATRII, ET FILII, ET SPIRITUS SANCTII!
KZZZTKZZT

ZZZRP
ADIURO VOS... IN NOMINE... PATRII--

OOF

HONEY? YOU FAINTED AGAIN--COME BACK TO US, POOPSIE!
FWUMP
WHAT THE FUCK WAS THAT?
I WOULD SAY AN APPARITION OF SORTS, BUT WHETHER IT IS AN ENERGETIC DISTURBANCE TAKING HUMAN FORM TO COMMUNICATE WITH US, OR A LEGITIMATE HUMAN SOUL, I CAN'T SAY.
UH-HUH. I DON'T FUCK WITH GHOSTS.

MA'AM? WHAT IS THAT DEVICE?
SACRIMETER. SUCKS UP GHOSTS. IT'S BEEN PRIMED WITH ALL OF THE GHOSTS IT'S SUCKED UP BEFORE. LIKE HOW A FLYTRAP WORKS BETTER AFTER IT'S CAUGHT A FEW FLIES.
LIKE ATTRACTS LIKE. THAT'S JUST PHYSICS.

AND CLEANUP IS SO EASY!
JUST A LITTLE TUG AND THE SPIRIT IS FILTERED THROUGH BLESSINGS AND DISPERSED ENERGETICALLY, TO RETURN TO PURGATORY.
I DON'T FUCK WITH GHOSTS...
PIFF

...GONNA GO FIND THE DOG.

THE GHOST THING ISN'T A THING, THERE ISN'T REALLY A SPECIFIC REASON FOR IT.
POOOOOCH!
HERE BOY!
THEY'RE JUST ALL INVASIVE AND OVERLY EMOTIONAL IN PUBLIC, IT MAKES ME UNCOMFORTABLE...
MAYBE I'M SAYING MORE ABOUT MYSELF THAN I AM GHOSTS, HERE.
IF YOU COME BACK, I'LL LET YOU EAT FROM DARIO'S LITTER BOX? EHHH?
I CAN'T HIT THEM WITH MY BAT SO I DON'T LIKE THEM, OKAY?
SIMPLE AS THAT.
POOCH!
POOOOOCH?

EHHHH...
HEEHHH...
DRIP

WHY DIDN'T I BRING A LIGHT...
HOLD ON, BOY, I SEE YOU! I'M COMING TOWARDS THE LIGHT!

GOD, I SHOULD BE SO LUCKY.

UH, POOCH OL' BOY?
WANNA...

...GIMME...
...THAT...
...SPOTLIGHT?

OOOOOOOOOOOOO...
OH NO, FUCK NO, FUCK THIS BLUE PLANET SHIT!

AT LEAST I HOPE IT'S BLUE PLANET.

I DON'T WANNA THINK ABOUT WHAT ELSE YOU'VE BEEN WATCHING WHERE YOU CATCH GIRLS IN YOUR TENTACLES.
GNASH

HUP!

WHAT DID I FUCKING TELL YOU?!
GHOSTS!
WHOOSH

AT LEAST THIS ONE'S DUMB AS A FISH.
HEADS UP!

HEYYY, YOU MIGHT WANNA WARM UP YOUR SACRED-O-METER, BEC--
AH.
I HAD HOPED BOTH THE DOGS WOULDN'T BE AN ISSUE.
NO MATTER AT ALL.
MMPH!
I CAN USE YOU.

YOUR FRIEND IS THE MAIDEN, WITH HER SEEKING NATURE.
WITH MY GIFTS AND NURTURING NATURE, I OF COURSE AM THE MOTHER.

AND YOU, CASSANDRA, PROPHETESS, YOU ARE LACHESIS, THE KILLER, THE DEATH-CRONE--

OOF!

THE FUCK IS THIS?!
WHAT ARE YOU DOING TO CAT?
WHAT HAPPENED TO YOUR DOCUMENTARY?
IT'S ACTUALLY MORE OF A GENRE DOCU-SERIES...

YOU HAVE TEN SECONDS TO EXPLAIN BEFORE I HANG YOU FROM THAT THONG.
EHH... IT'S ELAINE'S IDEA! I'M JUST THE FACE OF THE OPERATION!

UGH, BAD NEWS FOR YOUR OPERATION.
HEY, CAT, THESE ARE STANDARD CREEPS, I'VE DEALT WITH A TON.
LET'S GET YOU OUT BEFORE YOU GET SACRIFICED, HONEY.

WHERE'S POOCH?!
YOU WERE GONNA FIND HIM!
YEAH, UH, I'M WORKING ON IT.
YOU GIRLS STILL DON'T UNDERSTAND?

WE ARE DEMONOLOGISTS.
NOT DEMON HUNTERS. WE INVESTIGATE, NOT EXTERMINATE.
AND IF IT'S SOMETHING USEFUL... WE HAVE THE MEANS TO TRAP IT.
THIS ENTIRE HOUSE LIES ON A POWERFUL SOURCE OF SPIRITUAL ENERGY... AND WE INTEND TO TRAP IT. FOR A RAINY DAY.

KZKT
KZT
AND USE IT FOR OUR OWN NEEDS.

OH NO.
DID I STILL DO THE RIGHT THING IN ASKING YOU TO COME ALONG?
I'M GONNA PUT THAT GAG BACK ON YOU--

YOU FOOLISH GIRLS.
WE CONTROL THE SUPERNATURAL EVERYWHERE WE GO. IT'S OUR BUSINESS. DEMONS? GOD? WITCHES?
WE BELIEVE IN THE ALMIGHTY DOLLAR.

AND OUR GOD WANTS SACRIFICE.

CHOOSE WHICH ONE OF YOU DIES.

SPLUT
HURK--!

OH, I HAVE.
WITH SUCH A POWERFUL **MAIDEN** AND **CRONE** HERE IN THIS POWERFUL PLACE, WHY WOULD I SACRIFICE EITHER?

THANK YOU, LOYAL SERVANT.
YOU WILL ENTER MY HALLOWED HALL OF HUSBANDS.

WE AREN'T DOING YOUR RITUAL, NO MATTER WHAT!
POOCH RAN AWAY! YOU MADE MY FRIEND--
DOG.
WELL, HE'S REALLY MORE THAN A *DOG*--

SILENCE!
YOU MUST BE ***PRESENT***--NOT ***WILLING.***

HELL WITH EITHER.
CAT, LET'S GET OUT OF HERE!

OH, I DON'T THINK SO...

GIRLS, YOU DON'T UNDERSTAND.
I HAVE SUCH--
CASSIE!

SIGHTS--ACKK-- TO SHOW US.
YEP-- HURK!-- OFFERING US POWER--

LADY, I MAY NOT HAVE SPELLS, OR A BAT, OR EVEN MY DOG...

...BUT YOU CAN KISS *THESE FISTS!*

BAP
BAP
CAT--

IT IS THE NATURE OF THE MAIDEN TO HATE AND FEAR THE MOTHER.
NO MATTER. YOU AND THE CRONE ARE HERE.
THE SACRIFICE IS PREPARED.

THE RITUAL CAN BEGIN. SOON ALL THE LEY ENERGY OF THE DEMARCO HOUSE AND THESE WOMEN WILL--

WHAT--?!
Snrff snarf Snarf

GULP
MMMMM... FLESHMEATS!

MONGREL! YOU ATE THE SACRIFICE!
POOCH! YOU'RE SAFE!
I THOUGHT YOU'D GOTTEN LOST!
PET MEEE...

CASSIE?!
VLAD! BUDDY! WE'RE OKAY, I THINK!
ALL THAT ENERGY... DRAINED FROM ME... FOR NOTHING...

CAT, BUDDY, I'M SORRY YOU DIDN'T GET YOUR SCOOP.

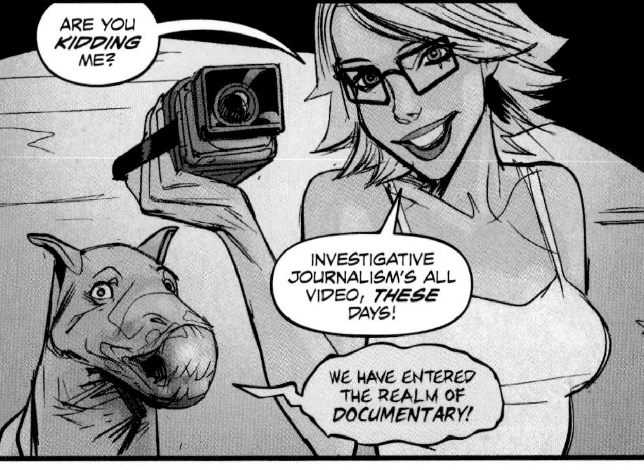
ARE YOU KIDDING ME?
INVESTIGATIVE JOURNALISM'S ALL VIDEO, THESE DAYS!
WE HAVE ENTERED THE REALM OF DOCUMENTARY!

WELL, VLAD, THAT BURROUGHS GUY IS DEAD AND THE LADY WON'T BE BEWITCHING ANYONE FOR A *WHILE.*
BONUS-- WE HELPED CAT, AND POOCH DIDN'T DIE.
CAT WASN'T EVEN *THAT* ANNOYING THIS TIME.
ALSO SHE SURVIVED. THAT IS GOOD.
WELL DUH, VLAD.
HEY, YOU'RE NOT MAD YOU KINDA HAD TO SIT THIS ONE OUT, ARE YOU?
MM?
BAP
NNOOO.
THE ELAINE WOMAN WAS GIVING ME THE *EVIL EYE.*
SHE SAID SHE WANTED ME TO *POSSESS* HER.
UHHH...
TONIGHT! FOUND FOOTAGE HORROR FESTIVAL: CAT CURIO'S THE BURROUGHS INVOCATION.
TOMORROW: TOY, DOG, AND COMIC SHOW!
NEXT MONTH: HACK/SLASH: RESURRECTION #8: RETURN TO HAVERHILL!
SHE SAID SHE WANTED ME... *INSIDE* HER?
OH BOY, BUDDY.
THAT'S *NOT* WHAT THAT MEANS.
-fin-

ISSUE 8 COVER BY
TIM SEELEY & ADDISON DUKE

ISSUE 8 COVER B BY
DANIELLE OTRAKJI

HEY, LEMME GET, UH...
FOOD BREAK.
I'LL BE WITH YOU SHORTLY.
I GET DEMONIC WHEN I'M HUNGRY.

...TWO DIABLO BURRITOS, A THELEMADILLA, CHIPS AND AN ANTON LAVERDE SALSA, AN ORDER OF ILLUMINATI QUESO TRIANGLES, A LARGE BA'AL BLAST, AAAAND--

IF I GET A CINNAMON BAPHOMET WILL YOU EAT HALF?
I CAN NEVER FINISH THE HORNS.
YES. BUT ALSO HOT SAUCE. SEVENTH LEVEL.

AAAAND A CINNAMON BAPHOMET.

SAUCE ME A SACRIFICE, MY DUDE.

HAVERHILL
NEXT EXIT
'CAUSE IT'S THE LAST BITE OF DELICIOUS CHAIN-RESTAURANT EVIL YOU GET BEFORE WE ENTER--
THE WHOLESOME AMERICANA MILKSHAKE ZONE!

HAMBURGERS
HOT DOGS
SHAKES
FRIES
OKAY, HI, BETTER NOW!
MY BELLY IS FULL OF THE PLEASANT SPICY BURN OF THE DAMNED.
AND I'M SEEING ABOUT SOME OLD PLACES. SINCE I'M STARTING TO FEEL A LITTLE GUILTY ABOUT LEAVING PLACES A BURNING HOLE IN THE GROUND.

SOME PLACES ARE TENACIOUS ENOUGH THAT THEY GROW BACK, EVEN AFTER I DO MY VERY BEST TO RUIN THEM.

AFTER YOU, MY DUDE.
HAVERHILL'S ONE OF THOSE PLACES. TIMELESS.
PRISTINE.
NAIVE TO A FAULT.

OR SO IT WAS?
WHAT THE HELL?!
SMELLS LIKE SOUR MILK AND BURNING FAT IN HERE.
REMINDS ME OF HOME.
$5

WHAT *HAPPENED* TO THIS PLACE?
I WOULDN'T DRINK A MILKSHAKE HERE IF YOU *PAID* ME!

ICE CREAM MACHINE'S BROKEN, NO MILKSHAKES!
I *SAID* I DIDN'T *WANT* ONE, *JEEZ.*
WHERE ARE ALL THE IRRITATING LITTLE MALT-SHOP SWEETIES AND THEIR STUPID ANNOYING LOVE TRIANGLES?

DID YOU PEOPLE SOMEHOW GET AS SHITTY AS THE REST OF THE WORLD?!
WHEN DID YOU START SMOKING INSIDE?
IF YOU DON'T *LIKE IT*, CITY MOUSE, YOU CAN *GIT!*

FINE, YOU LOWLIFES AREN'T THE REASON I CAME TO HAVERHILL ANYWAY!

IF I WANTED TO BE DEPRESSED SOMEWHERE THAT SMELLED LIKE GARBAGE, I'D STAY IN MY DAMN TRUCK!
HAVERHILL

THIS SEEMS... ***WHOLESOME***.
HISTORY FESTIVAL
PRESENTED BY THE HAVERHILL HIGH STUDENT BODY
WITH SPECIAL THANKS TO THE CHANDERS FAMILY
DISCOVER YOUR ROOTS
REMEMBER THE FOLKS
10-3

YEAH!
ANNOYINGLY SO.
LET'S CHECK IT OUT.
SATURDAY, 10-3
ENCOURAGED.

YES. YESSS.
THIS IS THAT BALM FOR THE SOUL I NEED.
THEY'RE SO GOOD AND PURE IT MAKES ME FEEL BAD ABOUT MYSELF.

IT'S PERFECT, VLAD!
LOOK AT THESE NERDS! THEY'RE SO HAPPY!

I DIDN'T RUIN IT, VLAD!
WE LEFT AND IT'S STILL FINE!
UM, EXCUSE ME?

HOLY DISCOUNT BODY SPRAY AND PRESSED KHAKIS, VLAD!
WOULD YOU LIKE TO SUBMIT YOUR DNA FOR ANCESTRY TESTING?
WE TAKE JUST THE TINIEST AMOUNT OF BLOOD.

AH, NOT THAT VEIN. IT'S A FAKE.
DON'T WORRY ABOUT IT, IT WAS FOR A... THING.
SO, HEY, THIS HISTORY FESTIVAL IS PRETTY, UH, POPPIN'?

NOT LIKE IT USED TO BE.

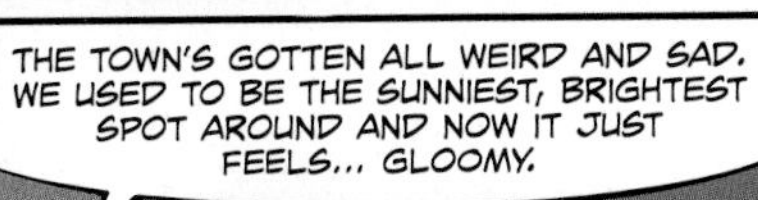
THE TOWN'S GOTTEN ALL WEIRD AND SAD. WE USED TO BE THE SUNNIEST, BRIGHTEST SPOT AROUND AND NOW IT JUST FEELS... GLOOMY.

LAST NAME, FIRST NAME?
HACK, CASSIE--

I THOUGHT THAT WAS YOU!
I'M CHET CHANDERS! I WAS JUST A KID WHEN YOU AND VLAD WERE HERE BEFORE, BUT I KNEW LUNK AND TRISH AND ALL OF THOSE GUYS!

YEAH, SPEAKING OF WHICH, WHERE ARE THOSE GUYS?
THIS DOESN'T SEEM LIKE THE SORT OF TOWN WHERE PEOPLE GROW UP AND MOVE AWAY...

THEY DID JUST THAT.
THIS PLACE HAS CHANGED, CASSIE. IT'S WEIRD. I FEEL LIKE I DON'T FIT IN.
I DIDN'T LOSE MY LIGHT WHEN EVERYONE ELSE DID.

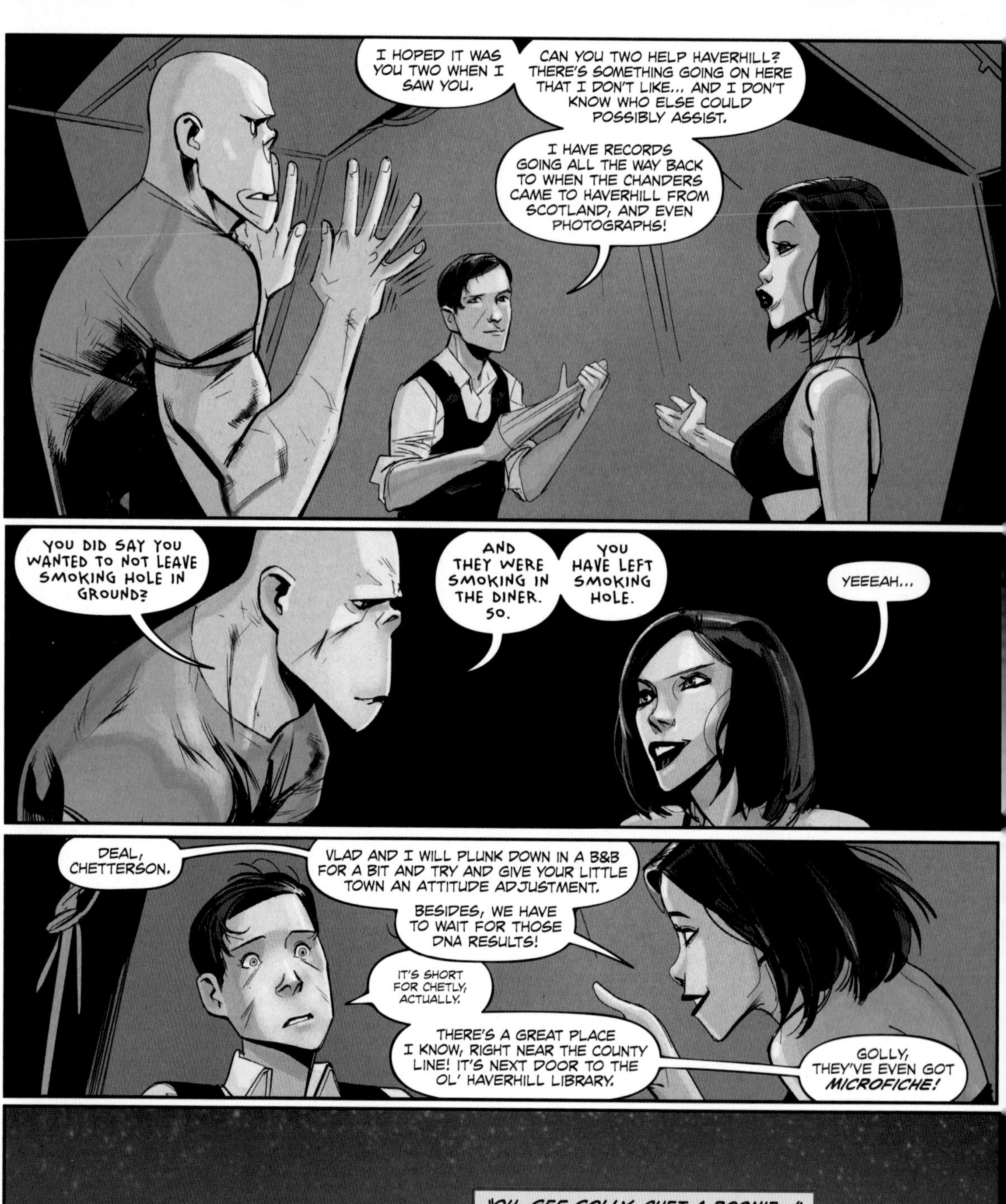
I HOPED IT WAS YOU TWO WHEN I SAW YOU.
CAN YOU TWO HELP HAVERHILL? THERE'S SOMETHING GOING ON HERE THAT I DON'T LIKE... AND I DON'T KNOW WHO ELSE COULD POSSIBLY ASSIST.
I HAVE RECORDS GOING ALL THE WAY BACK TO WHEN THE CHANDERS CAME TO HAVERHILL FROM SCOTLAND, AND EVEN PHOTOGRAPHS!
YOU DID SAY YOU WANTED TO NOT LEAVE SMOKING HOLE IN GROUND?
AND THEY WERE SMOKING IN THE DINER. SO.
YOU HAVE LEFT SMOKING HOLE.
YEEEAH...
DEAL, CHETTERSON.
VLAD AND I WILL PLUNK DOWN IN A B&B FOR A BIT AND TRY AND GIVE YOUR LITTLE TOWN AN ATTITUDE ADJUSTMENT.
BESIDES, WE HAVE TO WAIT FOR THOSE DNA RESULTS!
IT'S SHORT FOR CHETLY, ACTUALLY.
THERE'S A GREAT PLACE I KNOW, RIGHT NEAR THE COUNTY LINE! IT'S NEXT DOOR TO THE OL' HAVERHILL LIBRARY.
GOLLY, THEY'VE EVEN GOT MICROFICHE!

"OH, GEE GOLLY, CHET-A-ROONIE..."

...WHAT A QUAINT-ASS BED AND BREAKFAST YOU'VE LED US TO!
WE HAVE SLEPT IN WORSE.

SURE, BUT NOT HERE.

USUALLY THIS PLACE IS, YANNO. QUAINTER.
RRRING

HELLO...?
CASSIE!
I'VE GOT SOME GREAT NEWS, THERE'S ALREADY A RESULT ON YOUR DNA TEST!
DID YOU JUST... CALL ME ON THE HOTEL ROOM PHONE?

YEAH, IT'S QUAINTER.
LISTEN, IT LOOKS LIKE YOU HAVE SOME RELATIVES NEARBY ON YOUR MOM'S SIDE. CORDERO?
YEAH...?

NOT SHURE WHY THEY'D BE HERE, BUT I GOT A HIT THAT THERE'SH MORE INFO ON THEM...

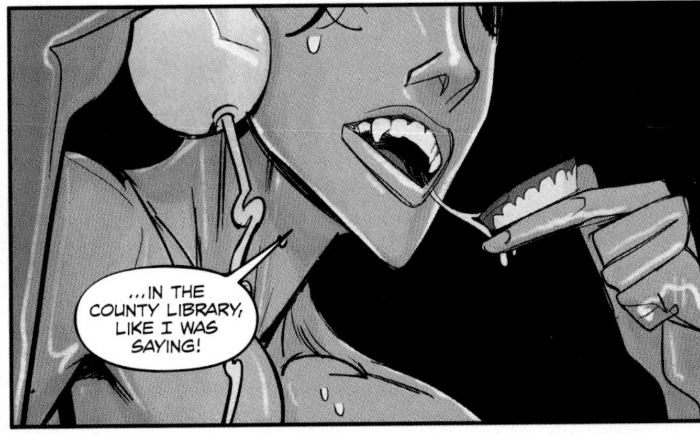
...IN THE COUNTY LIBRARY, LIKE I WAS SAYING!

MHM? REALLY?
I REALLY DO FEEL LIKE YOU'RE MEANT TO BE HERE, CASSIE!

IT JUST FEELS RIGHT.

OKAAAYY...
CLANGK

THIS FEELS A BIT... TIDY. NO?
RIGHT?

LIKE, HE HAPPENS TO PUT US UP IN A HOTEL RIGHT NEXT TO THE LIBRARY THAT HAS THE INFO?
WE WILL STAY FOR ONE NIGHT.
THEN WE CAN LEAVE SMOKING HOLE AND GO SOMEPLACE NEW, YES?

WORKS FOR ME.
FLICK

SLOSH SLOSH

SLOSH
EITHER THE WATER IN HAVERHILL IS REAL GROSS...

...OR THIS IS A BONA FIDE SEPIA-TONED HISTORICAL DREAM SEQUENCE.

COMPLETE WITH HISTORICALLY ACCURATE PAINFUL UNDERGARMENTS.
CORDERO!

THERE'S THAT NAME AGAIN.
HUH?
SHNK

HEH... HEH... HEH...
WANTED TO TEST YOUR REFLEXES!
VIAGO!
THAT'S HIS NAME.
I KNOW HIM.
LET'S HEAD TO THE DOCKMASTER.

I HAVE BUSINESS AT THE DOCKS.
I'M SURE I DO, IN THAT WAY THAT YOU ONLY KNOW THESE THINGS IN DREAMS.

NOK NOK NOK

'LO.
I HAVE BUSINESS HERE. I THINK.
LAST NAME?
CORDERO. THAT'S ALL YOU NEED TO KNOW.
THAT'S ALL I KNOW, SO I HOPE IT'S ALL I NEED TO KNOW.

WANT I SHOULD BREAK IT--
CHUK-ATCH

C'MON IN.

MIND THE CANDLES.
CORDERO?

HERE YOU GO.

I'VE NEVER BEEN ABLE TO READ ANYTHING IN DREAMS.
I HEARD ONCE IF YOU CAN, IT MEANS YOU'RE A PSYCHOPATH.
AND STILL! NOTHING!

THAT WAS A JOKE, I'M NOT REALLY A PSYCH--

AAAAAAAAA--

--AAAAAAH!
AAAAAH!!

WHAT, UH--
GHK WHAT TIME IS IT?
UH...

FIVE?
YES? FIVE.
GET DRESSED.

BY THE TIME WE'VE GOT PANTS AND COFFEE...

"...THE LIBRARY WILL BE OPEN."
OKAY, COLDWELL, COLON?
VLAD, THIS DUDE'S LAST NAME WAS COLON...

FOUND IT!
COLON
CORDERO

HERE IT IS...
ONE CHRISTIANA CORDERO.
RECEIVING A SHIPMENT FROM PORT OF LEITH, EDINBURGH, FROM AN ***EARL OF CHANDERS***...

VLAD, WHAT ***THE FUCK?***
THIS IS OFFICIALLY ***PERSONALLY WEIRD.***
MAYBE IS WHY HE KNEW ABOUT YOU.
EXPLAINS THINGS.

BUT THEN WHY'D WE COME HERE UNLESS WE WERE ***CALLED BY CREEPY VAMPIRE MAGIC?***
THEY CAN DO THAT, YOU KNOW.
I THINK.

TALKS A BIG GAME, DESPITE DELIVERING NO KILLS.
LITTLE MISS
THE TOP OF THE CHARTS!
"I can't show you the bodies, they turned to ash, now get offa my lawn,"
IF WE LEAVE NOW, WE'VE GOT A FEW HOURS 'TIL THE SUN COMES UP.

"I'VE GOT A HUNCH ABOUT THAT PIER."

SOMETHING ABOUT THIS WATER...
I MEAN, BESIDES THOSE CREEPY DEEP ONES THAT WERE DOWN HERE LAST TIME WE WERE IN TOWN--
NO SWIMMING!

AAAH!

AAHAHA, KILL IT, VLAD, FUCKING KILL IT!!

HNNGH!
HISSSSS!
CRCOOOSH

THESE ARE... DEFINITELY NOT THE DEEP ONES FROM THE LAST TIME I WAS HERE.
SPLASH
NO SWIMMING

WHAP
RRRRREEEH!

DO NOT SNEAK UP ON ME!

SPLAK

VLAD!
EXECUTE TWO SCOOPS OF SHRAPNEL!
EHHH...

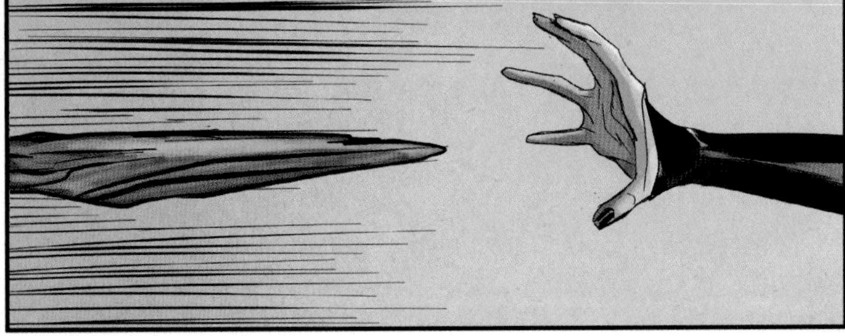

NO SWIMMING
SSSSS
WHUNK
EHHH...
THUKK
SSSSS
SSS...

I'M CALLING HER.

CALLING WH--

RRRING

OH! OH, YES, GOOD, OKAY.

DARK DESIRES, THANKS FOR CALLING. YOU'VE GOT VAMPI; WHAT CAN I DO FOR YOU?

HELLO? THE FUCK?

OH, HEY, CASS!
SORRY, YOU CAUGHT ME WORKING ON MY RADIO SHOW, I THOUGHT YOU WERE ONE OF MY CALLERS.
RADIO? ISN'T THAT A LITTLE... OUTDATED?
HONEY, I BOUNCE AROUND IN A CHERRY RED SLINGSHOT AND CHIPPENDALE'S CUFFS.
YOU THINK I GIVE A BAT'S ASS ABOUT OUTDATED?

FAIR.
HEY, LISTEN, ARE WE COOL? CAUSE I COULD USE SOME HELP.
I KEEP ENDING UP OUT OF MY ELEMENT LATELY. GHOSTS. VAMPIRES?

I'M SO EXCITED I'M NOT EVEN GOING TO BE UPSET YOU DIDN'T CALL ME ABOUT THE GHOSTS.
SEE YOU SOON! CIAO!

WAIT, I DIDN'T--
WE DIDN'T TELL HER WHERE WE WERE?

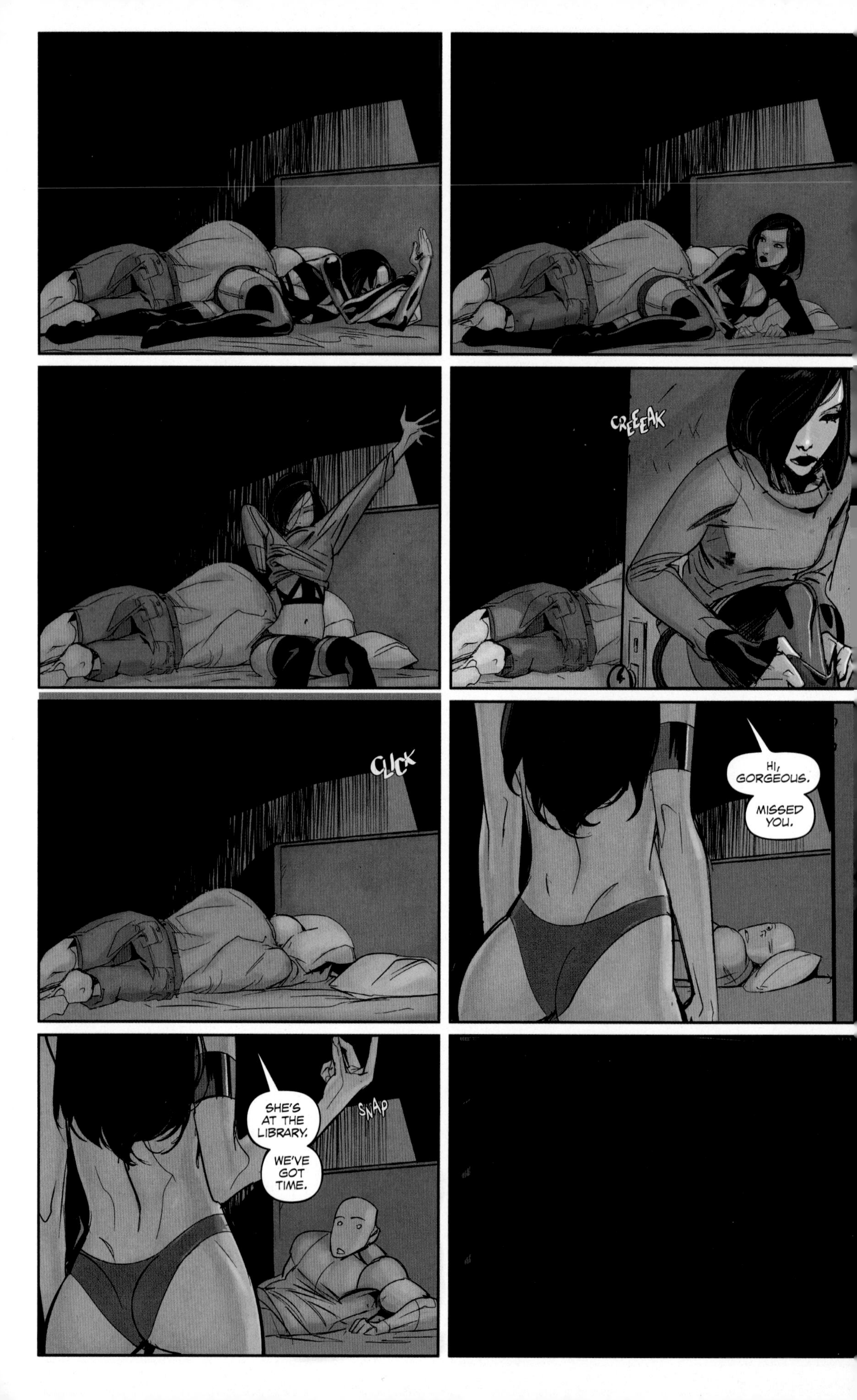
CREEEEAK
CLICK
HI, GORGEOUS.
MISSED YOU.
SHE'S AT THE LIBRARY.
WE'VE GOT TIME.
SNAP

I'VE NEVER BEEN MUCH OF A BOOKWORM.

BUT IT TURNS OUT IT'S A FANTASTIC WAY TO NOT BE ALONE WITH YOUR OWN THOUGHTS.
CASSIE?

ANYWAY, THOUGHTS ARE OVERRATED.
BE WITH YOU SHORTLY.
I HOPED YOU'D COME. I KNOW IT'S EARLY.
HAVERHILL HIGH

BUT I NEEDED YOU.

CHET!
UH, YEAH. DID... DID YOU CALL ME?
I DIDN'T EVEN CHECK MY PHONE, I JUST HAD A FEELING--

YOU'RE SO INTUITIVE...
...AND BEAUTIFUL...
HEY, SORRY TO INTERRUPT, I KNOW BRAINS AREN'T USEFUL AT MOMENTS LIKE THIS--

AND WARM...
LITERALLY NO ONE HAS EVER CALLED US WARM--

...UNLESS THEY WERE TRYING TO EAT US.
HISSSS!!
HGK!
PUT HER DOWN, PRIMETIME!
CASSIE!

SSUE 9 COVER BY
IM SEELEY & ADDISON DUKE

ALTERNATE COVER BY
JOE PEKA

SSSSSS...
OKAY, IF I'M BEING HONEST, I'M GLAD VLAD AND VAMPI SHOWED UP.

I DON'T MAKE MY BEST DECISIONS WHEN I'VE GOT A CUTIE BREATHING DOWN MY NECK.

BECAUSE, LIKE...
...WHAT A WAY TO GO.

FAH!
OOF!
CASSIE!

CORDERO WITCH!

YOUR COWARD'S CURSE KEEPS ME FROM TEARING INTO YOU LIKE YOU DESERVE.

HURK!

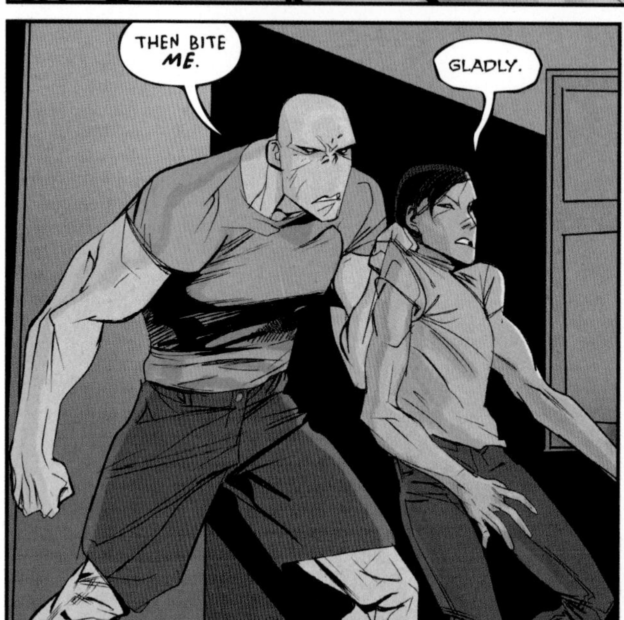
THEN BITE ME.
GLADLY.

AAUGH!
HEY!

I WAS SAVING THAT!

fbpt!

DARIO!
I'VE NEVER SEEN YOU MOVE THAT FAST, BUDDY!

HHHHH!
HHHHHHH!!
hsssssk!
?!

frOw!

SSSS...
HEY!
ASSHOLE, THAT'S MY CAT--!

UM...

WHUMP

HAVERHILL
COUNTY LINE

I MAY NOT HEAR YOU...
...AND I MAY NOT SEE YOU...

...BUT I SURE AS *HELL* CAN FEEL THE LITTLE HAIRS ON THE BACK OF MY NECK WHEN YOU'RE AROUND, BLOODSUCKER.

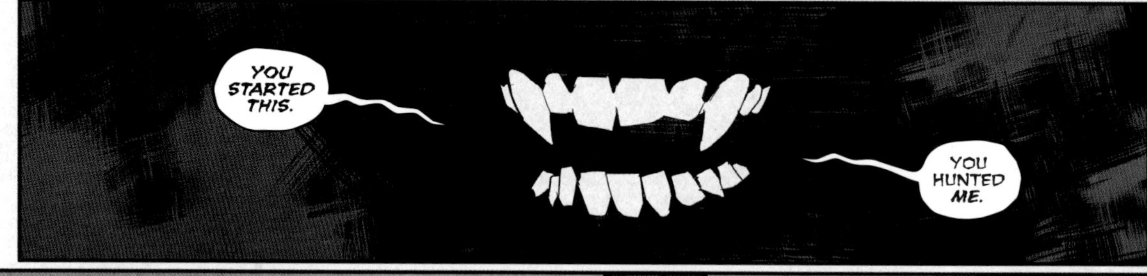
YOU STARTED THIS.
YOU HUNTED *ME.*

COME OVER THIS *COUNTY LINE* AND HUNT ME, *CORDERO.*

OR INVITE ME IN.
UNLESS YOU CAN'T TAKE ME WITHOUT YOUR LITTLE FRIEND VIAGO?
HE WAS DELICIOUS.
UGH!

EAT THIS!

HSSS--
THUK

HEH.
DON'T THINK I DON'T KNOW ABOUT THE STAKES...

HUP!
...THE HOLY WATER...

OOF!
IT'S NOT ENOUGH THAT YOU WON'T INVITE ME INTO YOUR TOWN, IS IT?
YOU HAVE TO COME HUNT ME HERE.

LISTEN, CHANDERS.

IF YOU THINK I'M JUST GONNA DIVE RIGHT BACK OVER THAT COUNTY LINE SO YOU CAN'T TOUCH ME...

...YOU'RE ABSOLUTELY RIGHT--

A SHAME I HAVE TO HAVE YOU FOR DESSERT, MISS CORDERO.

YOU'RE SO DAMN BITTER--
WAIT--!

DON'T!
WHY SHOULDN'T I?

YOU CAN HAVE HAVERHILL.

NICE TRY.
YOU CAN'T UNINVITE ME, AND I DON'T TRUST YOU FOR A SECOND.
I'LL LEAVE.

GIVE ME 'TIL SUNDOWN TOMORROW AND I'LL GET OUT.
HAVERHILL ISN'T WHAT IT USED TO BE--

THEY DON'T WANT A WOMAN LIKE ME AROUND ANYMORE.
IF HAVERHILL ISN'T MY HOME, I CAN'T KEEP YOU OUT OF IT.
I YIELD, CHANDERS. TAKE YOUR POUND OF FLESH AND LEAVE ME MINE. FEED ON WHOEVER YOU WANT, BUT LEAVE MY FAMILY ALONE.

AND I THOUGHT YOU WERE BITTER BEFORE...

NOTHING'S MORE BITTER THAN A COWARD!
AAAH-HAHAHA HAAA!

MMMH...

I'VE LEARNED TO LISTEN BEFORE OPENING MY EYES.

MMMM...

THIS HAPPENS TO ME MORE OFTEN THAN YOU'D THINK.

MORNING, SUNSHINE.
CARE TO JOIN US?
CASSIE!
YOU ARE AWAKE!
NO.

BE CAREFUL, YOU HAVE HEAD WOUND--
WELL, AT LEAST I KEPT MY SHIT TOGETHER IN FRONT OF A KITTY CAT.

OKAY, YOU KNOW WHAT?
IT'S A REFLEX. ALL VAMPIRES HAVE IT. CATS ARE CREEPY.

BESIDES, BIG BAD VLAD WAS HERE TO SAVE US.
AFTER CHET ALSO RAN FROM THE KITTY CAT. YES.

I HAD ANOTHER OF THOSE DREAMS, ABOUT MY MOM'S SIDE OF THE FAMILY.
I'M PRETTY SURE CHET IS SENDING THEM TO ME.

AND THERE'S ONLY ONE PLACE TO FIND YOUR OLD, WEIRD, RECLUSIVE, POSSIBLY RACIST RELATIVES...
Cordero

...SOCIAL MEDIA.

I WAS ABLE TO USE THE DNA TEST RESULTS AND SOME NON-SPECIFIC SEARCH-ENGINE-ING TO FIND THE ADDRESS OF MY CLOSEST LIVING RELATIVE-- CARAWAY CORDERO.

THESE THINGS, IT'S A LITTLE SCARY WHAT YOU CAN DO WITH THEM, YOU KNOW?
I MEAN, I LITERALLY HYPNOTIZE PEOPLE TO GET WHAT I WANT, SO...
NOK NOK

CREEEK

I SAID TO LEAVE THE CASHEW CHICKEN OUTSIDE AND GO SILENTLY.
WE HAVE NO CHICKEN.

I HAVE A ROOT BEER FLAVORED BARREL CANDY?
WAIT--
I THINK I'M RELATED TO YOU--!

I MEAN, I'M PRETTY SURE WE'RE RELATED, ACTUALLY.
THOUGH, I'M SURPRISED BY THE RECLUSIVE ATTITUDE.

I MEAN, YOU HAVE AN INSTAGRAM ACCOUNT.
I DON'T LIKE COMPANY.
THAT DOESN'T MEAN I DON'T HAVE INTERESTS.

SNF
I KNOW WHO YOU ARE.

I'M DE--
DELILAH'S DAUGHTER, YEAH, I CAN TELL.

YOU C'MON IN.

SORRY ABOUT THE MESS.
ARE YOU KIDDING?

THIS PLACE IS AMAZING!

OKAY, SETTLE DOWN.
JUST LEAVE A LIST OF WHAT YOU WANT WHEN I'M DEAD. I WANNA KNOW WHY YOU'RE HERE.
OH MAN, I TOTALLY WILL.

I CAN TELL FROM THE DECOR THAT IT'S NOT GOING TO FREAK YOU OUT TOO BADLY IF I START OUT BY TELLING YOU I'VE BEEN HAVING DREAMS ABOUT OUR SIDE OF THE FAMILY.
GO ON...

AND IF I THINK I'M BEING SENT SAID DREAMS BY A LOCAL VAMPIRE WHO HAS SOME SORT OF CURSE-GRUDGE AGAINST OUR FAMILY?
OF COURSE I'D BELIEVE YOU--

I'M THE ONE THAT CURSED 'IM.

BULLSHIT.
YOU'D HAVE TO BE, LIKE, A HUNDRED.
AND I SAW HOW MY MOM AGED, OKAY?
TERRIBLY. I'M GONNA HAVE A HUNCHBACK IF I LIVE TO BE THIRTY.

BELIEVE ME OR DON'T, CASSANDRA.
BUT YOU KNOW AS WELL AS I DO THAT THIS JOB...

...HUNTING LIKE WE DO...

...HAS A WAY OF AGING US IN SOME WAYS, AND KEEPING US YOUNG IN OTHERS.
HEAR, HEAR!

HONESTLY? I LOVE HER.
WELL, GORGEOUS, WHEN YOU GET TO BE MY AGE--

ACTUALLY I'M, LIKE, A THOUSAND, BUT THAT'S REALLY SWEET OF YOU.
YEAH, YEAH, SHE'S PRETTY COOL, EXCEPT--

EXCEPT FOR THE PART WHERE SHE SOLD OUT THE REST OF HAVERHILL TO A VAMPIRE TO SAVE HER OWN ASS.

IS THAT WHAT YOUR LITTLE DREAM TOLD YOU?
SURE DID.

YOUR MAMA'S MAMA WAS A LITTLE GIRL THEN.
I WANTED TO PROTECT HER, AND I DID.

BY LETTING A VAMPIRE TEAR ASS AROUND TOWN?
THAT TOWN DID FINE WITHOUT ME!
CLEARLY THERE HASN'T BEEN AN ISSUE!

WELL, THERE IS NOW!
WHEREVER THE FUCK THIS DUDE HAS BEEN, HE'S BACK NOW, AND THE DINER SMELLS LIKE OLD NASTY MILK AND ALL THE CUTE LITTLE GOODY TWO-SHOES KIDS LEFT.
IT'S WEIRD AND FUCKED UP AND I JUST WANNA FIX IT!

HUP!

CURSE WON'T BE AN ISSUE IF THE VAMPIRE'S DEAD. TAKE 'IM OUT.

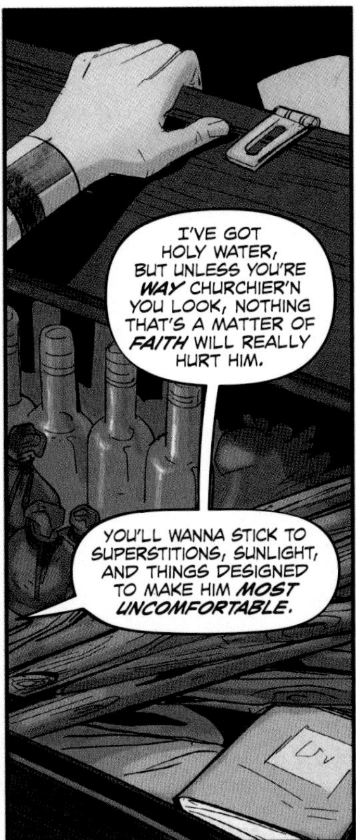
I'VE GOT HOLY WATER, BUT UNLESS YOU'RE *WAY* CHURCHIER'N YOU LOOK, NOTHING THAT'S A MATTER OF *FAITH* WILL REALLY HURT HIM.
YOU'LL WANNA STICK TO SUPERSTITIONS, SUNLIGHT, AND THINGS DESIGNED TO MAKE HIM *MOST UNCOMFORTABLE.*

THE GOOD NEWS ABOUT *STAKES* IS THAT EVEN IF THEY *DON'T* DO ANYTHING *FANCY* TO A VAMPIRE, YOU'RE STILL STABBIN' A GUY IN THE CHEST.
ANYTHING IS A STAKE. AN ARROW IS A STAKE. A CHAIR LEG IS A STAKE.

BE CREATIVE.
AND MAKE IT *HURT.*
HOLD ON, YOU'RE NOT COMING *WITH* US?
OH *HELL* NO, I'M RETIRED. NO THANKS.

ANYTHING I KILL I GOTTA HANG ON MY *WALL*, AND I *REFUSE* TO LOOK AT *THAT* MOTHERFUCKER AGAIN.
BUT HAVE FUN, AND *REMEMBER...*

...IT'S NOT SO MUCH A *CURSE* AS A *RESTRAINING ORDER*, SO IF *YOU* ATTACK *HIM* FIRST, DEAL'S OFF!

SLAM
BYE!

"OKAY, CHET WILL DEFINITELY BE HERE."
TONIGHT: HAVERHILL HERITAGE DANCE!

OH YEAH, VAMPIRES LOVE PROMS.
I HAVEN'T GOTTEN TO WEAR THIS DRESS SINCE MANSFIELD AND LAVEY'S SECRET WEDDING!
HHS
WELL ALSO, HE'S GOT EVERYONE THINKING HE'S SOME SORT OF GOODY TWO-SHOES NERD.

HE'S GOTTA KEEP UP APPEARANCES AMIDST THE MORTALS.
HEY, VLAD, SPEAKING OF NERD...

WHY ARE YOU DRESSED LIKE WE'RE ATTENDING THE DANCE, INSTEAD OF CRASHING IT TO SLAY A VAMPIRE?
VAMPI WANTED TO SEE ME IN A BOW TIE.
SHE SAID I WAS "JUICY."

OH, COOL, GREAT.
YOU AND VAMPI CAN GO GET HANDSY TO THE TOP TRACKS OFF NOW! THAT'S WHAT I CALL SAD 18 WITH THE OTHER MIDDLE SCHOOLERS.

LEAVE ROOM FOR JESUS, KIDS.

C'MON, WE GOT TIME FOR ONE SLOW GRIND BEFORE SHE NEEDS US.

IT MIGHT BE KIND OF A STRETCH, BUT HAVERHILL IS IMPORTANT TO ME.
I KNOW, NOTHING IS EVER IMPORTANT TO ME, IT'S MY THING, BUT THIS PLACE IS. IT WAS SO PURE.
MORE THAN I EXPECTED IT TO BE, ANYWAY.
SOMETHING ABOUT THESE PEOPLE AND PLACES I TREASURED AND HAD A HISTORY WITH, HAVERHILL, CAT, VLAD...
LOOK, AFTER EVERYTHING I'VE SEEN, I'M NEVER HAVING KIDS.
BUT IF I DID, I THINK IT MIGHT FEEL LIKE I FEEL ABOUT THOSE THINGS.
LIKE THE IDEA OF THEM BECOMING HARMED OR CORRUPTED IN SOME WAY...
...MAKES ME FEEL CRAZY ENOUGH TO COME BACK FROM THE FUCKING DEAD AND--

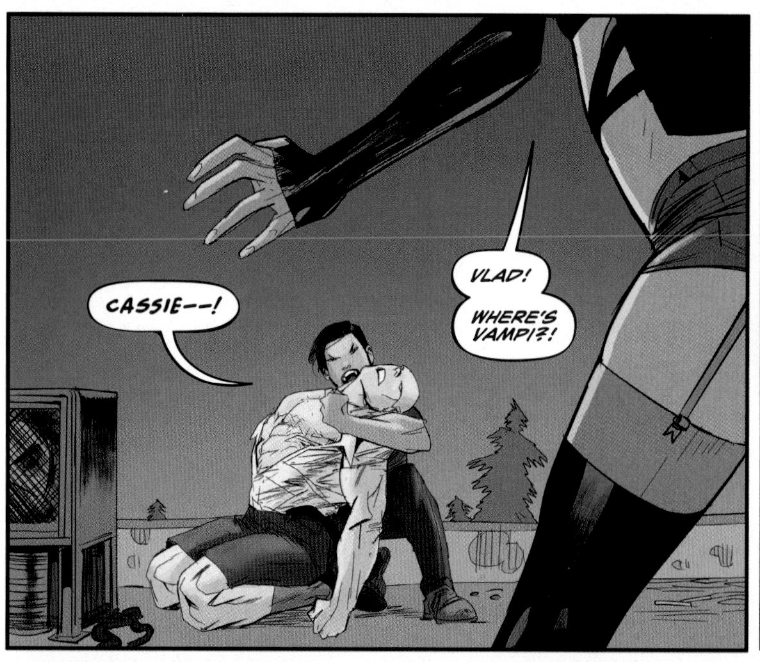
CASSIE--!
VLAD!
WHERE'S VAMPI?!

SHE--
FLEW OFF--

THAT'S WHY WE ALWAYS SAY, BUDDY...

...FRIENDS BEFORE CUTE REAR ENDS!
CASSIE-- NO!

IF YOU SWING AT HIM AND MISS THE CURSE WILL BREAK, HE WILL DESTROY YOU!

YOU HAVE TO JUST STRIKE AT HIM IN ONE--

KILL HIM--

IN--
ONE--

THUK

CASSIE--?

I'VE GOT GOOD NEWS AND BAD NEWS.

OKAY, GOOD NEWS FIRST.
A GIRL IN THE BATHROOM TOLD ME I WAS "GOALS."
BAD NEWS...

BAD NEWS IS THAT IF CHET WAS THE HEAD VAMPIRE, THE OTHERS WOULD HAVE ALL TURNED TO ASH WHEN YOU STAKED HIM.
THEY DID NOT TURN TO ASH.
NOPE. WHICH MEANS WE JUST KILLED SOME BIGGER, BADDER VAMPIRE'S FAAAAVORITE CUTE LIEUTENANT.
AND HE'S GOING TO BE PISSED.
OR SHE!
OR SHE.

ISSUE 10 COVER BY
RICHARD PACE

ALTERNATE COVER BY
JIM TERRY

CREEEAK

SSSSS...

HHHHH--
--HH!
Haverhill High
Heritage Award
goes to:
Chet Chanders

HSSSSSSSSS!!
WHUMP

INSOLENT CUR--

GKK--
YES--

--CALL ME CUR AGAIN, YOU WHELP--

SMASSH
THUK

DO YOU EVER HAVE THOSE NIGHTMARES WHERE YOU'RE BACK IN HIGH SCHOOL?
QUIT WITH THE HISSING, IT'S DUMB.
SSSS...

OH NO, THEY HAVE GOT MISTER GINSBERGER.
WHO?

I HAVE THOSE MORE THAN MOST PEOPLE.
THE MAN WHO TEACHES LIFE SCIENCES TO THE CHILDREN.
SHUNK

HOW COME YOU NEVER LEARN ANYONE'S NAME, CASSIE?

KEEPS THE BODY COUNT LOWER.
TRUST ME.
DO WE WANT TO HEAD BACK TO THE GYM?
I REQUESTED "PONY" AND I THINK THEY'RE GONNA PLAY IT ANY MINUTE NOW.

HONESTLY I'M MORE SCARED OF THE DANCING THAN I AM THE MONSTERS, AND I THINK WE ALL KNOW THAT.
NICE TRY.
NOW'S WHEN VLAD AND I ACTUALLY NEED THOSE THOUSAND-YEAR-OLD ALIEN VAMPIRE QUEEN POWERS THAT YOU SUPPOSEDLY HAVE.

WELL, YOU KNOW LIKE I DO THAT WE'VE CLEARLY GOT AN ELDER VAMPIRE TO CONTEND WITH.
THE CHET-WAS-A-CUTE-LIEUTENANT-TO-ANOTHER-VAMPIRE THEORY I EARLIER POSTULATED.
I PREFER CUTE-TENANT THEORY, BUT YES.

HNNNNHHH...
WE SHOULDN'T HAVE TO TAKE OUT ALL OF THESE VAMPIRES INDIVIDUALLY.
IN FACT, IF WE'RE ABLE TO DISPATCH THE ELDER VAMPIRE, MOST OF THESE FOLKS SHOULD TURN BACK TO NORMAL.
MAYBE.
SO, WE'LL FIND HIM.
OR HER.
OR HER.

YANK
HSSS!

BY MY COMMAND, LEAD US TO YOUR MASTER.

GOD DAMNIT, VAMPIRELLA!

YOU HAD TO PICK A VARSITY TRACK STAR?

OH, C'MON, RUNNING'S GOOD FOR YOUR HEART!
RIGHT? IS THAT WHAT YOU HUMANS USE FOR RUNNING? HEARTS?

THOSE--
--ARE-- LEGS.

CAN WE--
HNNGH
--STOP FOR A MINUTE?

I'VE EATEN--
HHK!
--A LOT OF COMBO MEALS LATELY.

WHOOF!
WHAP

HNNNGH--

I DON'T EVEN TRY TO STOP MYSELF.

CASSIE, NO!
I KNOW, ON SOME LEVEL, I SHOULDN'T JUST BEAT THEM INTO A PULP.

IF WE FOCUS ON THE ELDER VAMPIRE, THESE FOLK WILL ALL TURN BACK TO NORMAL, AND THEY SHOULD BE ABLE TO DO THAT WITHOUT BROKEN CLAVICLES.
SO IF I KNOW THAT, THAT BEGS THE QUESTION...

WHAT IS WRONG WITH YOU, LATELY?
...WHAT IS WRONG WITH ME, LATELY?
JESUS, HE WAS GONNA BITE YOU...

SUCH A SOFTIE THESE DAYS.

SEVERAL HOURS LATER.
DUDE.
NOOO NO NO NO!
HEHHH...
TAK TAK TAK TAK TAK

HUK--
WHOOOSH

HIDEOUS MORTAL--
WE HAVE BEEN WALKING AROUND THIS TOWN FOLLOWING RANDOM VAMPIRES FOR HOURS.

SSSS!
NONE OF THEM HAVE LED US TO THE LEADER, AND THERE'S NO SIGN OF VAMPIRELLA.
I THINK SHE DITCHED US.
WHUMP

I GUESS... I WAS LITTLE BIT HOPING...
OH.
YOU SAVED MY LIFE, HOW CAN I REPAY--

FUCK OFF, MY FRIEND IS HAVING GIRL TROUBLES.
NNRRF!
BUDDY.
I KNOW. "FRIENDS BEFORE CUTE REAR ENDS," BUT...
...I LIKE HER.

VLAD, LISTEN.
SHE IS A THOUSAND-YEAR-OLD VAMPIRE ALIEN QUEEN.

AND I KNOW A LOT OF THOSE TRAITS WERE ON YOUR "IDEAL PARTNER" LIST.
BUT I THINK MAYBE YOU TWO JUST WANT DIFFERENT THINGS.

LIKE, YOU DON'T WANT TO SUFFER.
AND SHE...

...I THINK SHE EXPLICITLY GETS OFF ON SUFFERING?
HEY, YOU GONNA TELL ON ME IF I BREAK A FEW OF THESE VAMPIRE KNEECAPS?
NO.
I AM IN BAD MOOD NOW BECAUSE OF GIRL.

AHHHHHHHH...

LOOKS LIKE SOMEONE'S GETTING A CALL FROM YOUR GIRLFRIEND.
RUDE.

MAYBE IT ISN'T HER CALLING THEM.
IS THIS YOU BEING CAUTIOUS ABOUT WHAT COULD BE IN THERE?
OR IS THIS YOU HOPING YOUR GIRLFRIEND ISN'T CALLING ALL THESE OTHER VAMPIRES INSTEAD OF CALLING YOU UP?

YOU ARE SO VERY MEAN WHEN YOU ARE NOT HAVING GIRLFRIEND OR BOYFRIEND.
THAT'S NOT IT--

THEN WHAT IS IT?
OH LOOK, VAMPIRES, A DISTRACTION!

AREN'T WE SUPPOSED TO BE GOOD TO THEM FOR WHEN THEY TURN BACK?
OH, IT'S JUST SOME BROKEN BONES.
VAMPIRES CAN HEAL FROM THOSE, AND BESIDES, SOME OF THESE VAMPIRES ARE STUDENT ATHLETES.

THEY'VE SEEN WORSE.

HEHH...
Y'ALL AREN'T THE TALKY TYPE OF VAMPIRES, I'VE NOTICED.

FINE BY ME.

DESPITE THE ATTIRE, I DON'T REALLY GO IN FOR GOTH POETRY.

HGGHH--
I'M MORE OF A LOUD, STUPID BUTT ROCK KINDA GAL.
NO.
NO MORE.
THUKK

NO MORE SINGING DEF LEPPARD IN THE TRUCK, CASSIE!!

?!
?!

AAAGHGH!
GHHGGHHGH...
SNF
HOLY WATER?
NAH.
CAT PEE.

CARAWAY WAS RIGHT ABOUT THE HOLY WATER BEING BULLSHIT, BUT EVERYONE HATES A MOUTHFUL OF CAT PEE.
ESPECIALLY VAMPIRES.
THAT'S FOUL.

HELLO, VAMPIRELLA.
OH, HI THERE; YOU FELT LIKE SHOWING UP?
I FOUND WHERE THE ELDER VAMPIRE'S BEEN STAYING, ACTUALLY.

HEY THERE, KID.
YOU LOOK GOOD.
OH YEAH?

YEAH, THE CREEP'S BEEN CAMPING OUT...
CREEEK

...IN TRISH'S BEDROOM.
WHOA, EW!

WHAT A WEIRD PLACE TO--

HOLD ON, DOES TRISH STILL LIVE HERE?
BECAUSE--
HHN--

HOLY SHIT, TRISH?!
OH MY GOD, C-C-CASSIE?

I'D HEARD YOU WERE DOING A LITTLE EAT, PRAY, LOVE ROAD TRIP!
I PRAYED MYSELF, THAT YOU'D COME SAVE HAVERHILL!

UH, YEAH, I'M HERE TO HELP...
WHAT ARE YOU STILL DOING HERE?
THAT VAMPIRE GUY, CHET, SAID THAT YOU AND LUNK, YOU WERE ALL GONE.
OH, CASSIE.

LUNK IS GONE. HE DIDN'T MAKE IT.
DIDN'T MAKE IT...

...HOW?

WELL CASSIE, THERE'S BEEN SO MANY HORRIBLE THINGS HERE, WE CAN'T SAY.

AND THIS AWFUL ELDER VAMPIRE HAS HAD ME CAPTURED HERE AGAINST MY WILL, SO--
WHAT DO THEY LOOK LIKE?
HM?

THE ELDER VAMPIRE.
OR HER.
YOU SAW HIM!

WHAT ARE YOU IMPLYING?
NOTHING.
HEY, YOU'RE NOT WEARING YOUR CLASS RING.
SO?

THEY'RE NICE RINGS.
PURE SILVER.

CATCH!

AAAAAAAGH!
CURSE YOU FUCKING CORDERO HUNTERS AND YOUR TRICKSSSSS--
OOOF!
VLAD! VAMPI!
TRISH IS THE LEAD VAMPIRE, FUCKIN' STAKE HER!

CASSIE!
HNNGH!
VLAD!!

FRIENDS BEFORE--

SLEEP.

GOD, YOU'RE THE WORST KIND OF GIRLFRIEND!
I WANT TO BE FRIENDS WITH YOU, BUT YOU'RE MAKING THAT REALLY HARD!

DON'T YOU GET IT, CASSIE?
WHAT HAVERHILL REALLY NEEDS...

...IS IMMORTALITY.
...IS IMMORTALITY.
OH, YOU'RE KIDDING ME.

LET ME GUESS, HERE COMES A SPEECH ABOUT HOW YOU MADE THE CHOICE TO BECOME A VAMPIRE, YOU DIDN'T FEEL PRESSURE ABOUT AGING--

SILENCE.
I'D HEARD YOU CORDEROS WERE MOUTHY. I HAD NO IDEA.
WHACK

HOW ARE YOU THE ELDER VAMPIRE IF CHET IS, LIKE, A HUNDRED YEARS OLD?
WAIT, YEAH, EXPLAIN THAT.

THE POWER OF THE BLOOD EXCHANGE IS ANCIENT, DARK MAGIC.
CHET WAS THE ELDEST AMONG US, YES, AND OUR LEADER AT FIRST... BUT HE BELIEVED IN MY CAUSE.
HAVERHILL WAS ONCE AN IDYLLIC SLICE OF AMERICANA, BUT NOW IT HAS BECOME... DRAB. FILTHY.
SINCE YOU CAME, YOU BROUGHT WITH YOU YOUR FOUL LANGUAGE, YOUR FILTHY HABITS.

YOU INTRODUCED YOUR DISEASE AND YOU MADE MY SWEET, RIPE TOWN TURN TO ROT.

I KNEW THAT AS VAMPIRES, WE COULD PRESERVE WHAT WAS LEFT OF HAVERHILL.
SO, IN THE DARKEST RITUAL, WITH THE PUREST OF SACRIFICES, CHET TURNED HIS POWER OVER...

...TO ME.

SACRIFICES...
...LUNK?!

VAMPI, AND YOU'RE HELPING HER?
REALLY?!
LISTEN, KID.
I MAY NOT LOOK MY AGE, BUT I'VE BEEN HIKING FOR A THOUSAND YEARS.

I'M READY TO GO HOME, YOU KNOW?
OR AT THE VERY LEAST, MAKE ONE.

US GIRLS CAN HAVE OUR OWN LITTLE SLICE OF SUBURBAN PARADISE.
ALL IMMORTAL.
ALL OURS.
MOONBATHING BY THE POOL.

I'LL REMIND YOU THAT NO MATTER HOW SEXY THE CULPRITS...
...I AM STILL REALLY TRYING NOT TO GET BIT TO DEATH THIS WEEK.
THAT IS, ONCE WE TAKE OUT--

--THE LAST CORDERO VAMPIRE HUNTER!
AT LEAST THEY'RE WRONG ABOUT THAT.
I'M NOT THE LAST.

LET'S JUST HOPE SHE SHOWS UP.

SSUE 11 COVER BY
TIM SEELEY

ALTERNATE COVER BY
RICHARD PACE
PACE

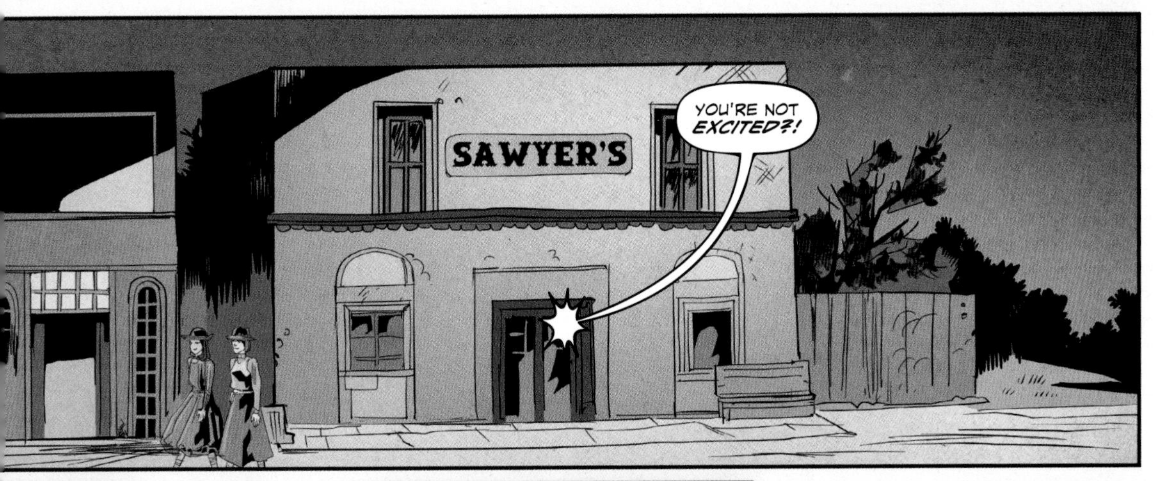
SAWYER'S
YOU'RE NOT *EXCITED?!*

VAMPIRES.
Y'AIN'T *EXCITED* TO HUNT VAMPIRES?
THEY ARE JUST PEOPLE... WITH TEETH, YES?
WHO BITE NECKS?
VAMPIRES ARE FUN BECAUSE THEY'VE GOT *RULES*, MY MAN.
THEY CAN'T ABIDE SUNLIGHT, FOR ONE.
IS IT SUNLIGHT? OR DAYTIME?
CAN THEY BE AWAKE IN THE DAY IN A DARK ROOM?
ALL DEPENDS ON WHO YA ASK.

SOME HATE RUNNING WATER, SOME CAN'T *ABIDE* GARLIC, AN' THEY PRETTY MUCH ALL HATE CATS.
CROSSES ARE A STICKY ONE--YOU GOTTA REALLY BELIEVE IN IT OR IT WON'T WORK, BUT YOU'RE TAKIN' A CHANCE THAT THE *VAMPIRE* EVEN KNOWS WHAT IT IS.
YOU GO TO SOME PART'A THE WORLD WHERE THEY AIN'T GOT *CHURCH* AND WAVE A *CROSS* AROUND, AND THEY'RE JUST GONNA STICK IT RIGHT THROUGH YA.

LOTTA FOLK UNDERESTIMATE THEM TEETH, THOUGH.
THEM DARK EYES.

ALL THAT IMMORTAL SMOOTH SKIN--
PARDON!

Y'ALL WANT ANOTHER ROUND?
NAH, WE OUGHTA BE HITTIN' THE DUSTY TRAIL.

TINK

SURE THING, BUDDY, I'LL MEET YA AT THE STABLES.

I GOTTA SEE A MAN ABOUT A HORSE, FIRST.

WHERE THE HELL'S VIAGO?
HEY, VIAGO, PINCH IT OFF, LET'S--
HHHHHHH...
KGH-- KGH--

MNNPH--

STILL 'BOUT THREE HOURS 'TIL SUNRISE.

I BET THAT GIRL AIN'T GOT THREE HOURS OF FIGHT LEFT IN 'ER.

LOOK AT ME NOW.
THE *JERSEY DEVIL* ONCE LOOKED ME IN THE EYES AN' *FILLED HIS PANTS* AND NOW I'M GETTIN' UP AT *FOUR IN THE GOT-DAMN MORNIN'* FOR...

...FUCKIN' *FAMILY SHIT.*

I DON'T MEAN TO BE RUDE, BUT I FEEL LIKE WE SPENT **WAY TOO MUCH TIME** AWAY BEFORE WE GOT BACK TO ME ABOUT TO BE RIPPED IN HALF BY THE BIG-BOOBED BABES OF VAMPIRE AMERICANA--

--BUT, BY ALL MEANS, HANG OUT WITH MY ABSENTEE GREAT AUNTIE INSTEAD--

KSSSH
--LET'S HOPE THAT'S HER NOW!

HSSSSS!
HNGH!
HISSSSSSS!

AUNT CARAWAY!
GET YOUR BOY AND GET ON DOWN.
VLAD'S ASLEEP, SHE PUT HIM IN SOME KIND OF TRANCE!

YOU'RE GONNA HAVE TO DRAG HIS BIG SLEEPIN' ASS OUT THE WINDOW, SWEETIE, THAT'S A VAMPIRE CURSE.
AW, MAN...

I GOT THEM VAMPIRES OFF YOUR ASS, DIDN'T I?!
C'MON-- HNNGH-- VLAD!

YOU'RE TOO GOOD FOR THIS, YOU STUPID PALOOKA.
SINCE WHEN ARE YOU HOOKING UP WITH GIRLS, ANYWAY?
TSSSH

I SHOULDA LET YOU GET STUCK BY THE GLASS AS PUNISHMENT.

OOH, I SHOULDN'T SAY THAT.
TUMP
TOO SLASHER-Y.

C'MON, MEATLOAF, SHE'S TALKIN' TO HERSELF UP THERE...

HEY, WAIT UP!
...BETTER GET ON BEFORE SHE CRACKS JUST LIKE HER MAMA.
RUDE.

WE BEST HOOF IT, THE FIRE'S GONNA MAKE ANY NESTING VAMPIRES IN THAT HOUSE SCATTER LIKE ROACHES.
BEST PART IS...

...I CAN STOP WASTIN' CROSSBOW BOLTS NOW, HEH.

THE SUN'S TURNIN' 'EM INTO JIFFY POP FOR ME!
UH HUH.

YOU'RE REALLY WORRIED ABOUT HIM, AREN'T YOU?
HE'S MY BEST FRIEND, CARAWAY.

WELL, HE'S SLEEPIN', HE AIN'T DEAD.

ONE MOMENT.

OH, DUDE, I CAN SMELL THAT FROM HERE...

BLEECCH--
HHHHNNH--
KOFF--
JESUS, CARAWAY, WHAT IS THAT STENCH?!
I THOUGHT THOSE WERE SMELLING SALTS!
HEH HEH...

...WEREWOLF TAMPON.
OLD CRYPTID HUNTIN' TRICK. YOU NEVER KNOW WHEN SOMETHIN' GROSS IS GONNA BE USEFUL.
HORRIBLE.
VLAD, YOU OKAY?

YES.
WHERE IS VAMPI?
THAT'S THE PROBLEM WITH THEM MONSTER WOMEN.
SHE WENT FERAL ON YA, BUDDY.

THEY MAY LOOK PRETTY, BUT DEEP DOWN, THEY AIN'T NO DIFFERENT FROM A TROPICAL FISH OR A POISONOUS PLANT.
PRETTY'S JUST ANOTHER WAY TO HUNT.

OKAY, BUT VAMPI IS OUR FRIEND.
IS SHE? DON'T LOOK LIKE IT TO ME.
SHE'S NOT LIKE TRISH.
FIRST OF ALL, SHE'S LITERALLY AN ALIEN, OR SOMETHING.
TRISH HAS TO HAVE VAMPIRELLA UNDER SOME KIND OF MIND CONTROL.
I KNOW VAMPIRELLA CAN DO THAT, I JUST DIDN'T THINK ALL VAMPIRES COULD.
THEY CAN'T.

BUT IF VAMPI AND TRISH DRANK EACH OTHER'S BLOOD, IT'S POSSIBLE THEY COULD SHARE POWERS, SHARE CONTROL, SHARE ALL SORTS OF THINGS.
SO, LIKE, TRISH COULD MASS MIND-CONTROL PEOPLE THAT AREN'T VAMPIRES NOW?
IF SHE WERE PRESENT IN FRONT OF A LOT OF PEOPLE?
A-YUP.
WHAT DAY IS IT?
HOW COME YOU NEVER KNOW THESE FACTS?
IT IS SUNDAY. I JUST WOKE UP AND I KNOW THIS.
I DON'T NEED JUDGMENT IN FRONT OF THE ANCESTOR, OKAY?
SUNDAY MEANS THE LAST NIGHT OF THE HAVERHILL HERITAGE FESTIVAL.
THE CARNIVAL. THE CARNIVAL.

HONESTLY, I'M SURPRISED THE CARNIVAL'S STILL GOING ON.
BETWEEN THE NEAR-CONSTANT VAMPIRE ATTACKS AND THE REVELATION THAT THE WHOLE EVENT'S LEAD ADVOCATE, CHET CHANDERS, WAS ACTUALLY AUNT CARAWAY'S LONG-TIME UNDEAD NEMESIS...

...I THOUGHT THEY'D CANCEL IT.
NOT THIS TOWN.

PART OF THE WAY THEY HIDE THE CORRUPTION, PLACES LIKE THIS ONE.
NO MATTER HOW BAD THINGS SEEM TO GET...

...IT'S BUSINESS AS USUAL 'ROUND HERE.
SO, HAVE YOU BEEN HERE THE OTHER TIMES I CAME TO HAVERHILL?
BECAUSE, LIKE, IT MIGHT HAVE BEEN USEFUL TO KNOW I HAD A WELL-ARMED RELATIVE IN THE AREA...

BLOOD'S JUST BLOOD.
NO ONE OWES ANYONE ANYTHING FOR IT.
BUT SPEAKIN' OF LADIES WHO SHARE BLOOD, I'M LOOKIN' TO PUT SOME VAMPIRE HEADS ON MY WALL, SO LET'S GET MOVIN'.

WAIT.
I NEED TO BE CLEAR, YOU'RE NOT KILLING VAMPIRELLA.
SHE'S MY FRIEND, AND VLAD'S...
...FRIEND, TOO.

I WORRY THAT IN A LIL BIT YOU'LL BE BEGGING ME TO DO EXACTLY THAT.
BUT DON'T LEMME SAY I TOLD YA SO.

I'M GONNA SET UP A PERIMETER 'ROUND THE CARNIVAL WITH THESE BAD BOYS, TO KEEP ANY VAMPIRES IN.
Y'ALL KEEP YOUR EYES OPEN.
OKAY.
SURE.

YOU WANNA PLAY CARNIVAL GAMES?
YES, ABSOLUTELY I DO.

YESSSSS!

ONE, PLEASE, FOR THE STRENGTH TEST GAME!

NO THANKS, WON'T NEED IT.
I BROUGHT MY OWN!

DANG!
HEY, LOOK AT THAT!
LITTLE LADY'S GOT AN ARM ON HER!

YEAH, AND *MOST* OF THE ARMS I KEEP ON ME ARE *MINE!*

DANG!

SHE'S GOT THAT CORDERO *ARM*.
BUT IF SHE'S PLAYING CARNIVAL GAMES WHILE I--
SSS...

HUP--
HISSSSS!

AAHH!
THUD
HHHH--!

THUK

HISSSSSS
FUCK OFF!

STUPID FUCKIN' SCRUB VAMPIRES.
SWEAR, IT'S LIKE SCARIN' POSSUMS.

ZRRRBT
ZRRRBT

Just scared some a them up your way, heads up for vampires
Y'all better not be playin those stupid ass carnival games! >:(

HEADS UP, VLAD--

FATHER, SAY A LITTLE PRAYER AND BLESS THESE WATER GUNS HERE FOR ME AND MY BRO, WON'T YOU?
UH, UH--?

ERM... BY THIS HOLY WATER AND BY YOUR PRECIOUS BLOOD--

--WASH AWAY ALL MY SINS O LORD?

SSSSSSSSSSSSSSSSSSSSSS!
PSSSSSH
PSSSSSH
YEAH, THAT'LL DO.
HEH HEH HEH.

HECK YEAH!
HEY!

OH, HEY.
THAT WAS PRETTY SWEET, THE WATER GUNS AND THE PRIEST AND ALL THAT--
I THINK I FOUND 'EM.
WHAT MAKES YOU THINK THAT?

HAUNTED HOUSE!
THIS SEEMS WAY TOO OBVIOUS...

CASSANDRA HACK.
WHEN LAST WE MET, I WAS NOT YET MY TRUE SELF.
AND YET...
YEAH, ABOUT THAT-- HOW ARE YOU THE HEAD VAMPIRE WHEN CHET WAS A VAMPIRE FOR WAY LONGER THAN YOU?

THE BLOOD CONTAINS MANY MAGICS.
CHET WAS MY VAMPIRIC SIRE, TRUE, BUT IN TIME I GREW MORE POWERFUL.

IN TIME, I WAS ABLE TO CONVINCE HIM TO FEED ME HIS OWN HEART IN A DARK RITUAL THAT ENABLED ME TO--
COOL. ANYWAY--

HISSS!
HNGH!

OOF
MM, HELL-O, YOU BEEFY PIEROGI.

NO. I DO NOT WANT TO BE YOUR PIEROGI ANYMORE!
YOU BETRAYED US FOR YOUR VAMPIRE FRIEND TRISH!
LET GO OF ME AND I'LL HELP YOU WITH HER!

HOW CAN I TRUST YOU?
YOU CAN'T, SUGAR.
BUT I DRANK HER BLOOD A FEW DAYS AGO AND I HAVEN'T SINCE. ALL THIS FIGHTING HAS BURNED IT OUT OF ME. LOOK, I'M SORRY I GOT WEIRD. I DON'T MEET OTHER CUTE GIRL VAMPIRES VERY OFTEN, OKAY?

BUT YOU'RE DEFINITELY A BETTER KISSER THAN HER.

SMASH
OOF!

I WON'T LET YOU TAKE THIS FROM US.
I KNOW I PEAKED IN HIGH SCHOOL, SO I PLAN TO STAY HERE FOREV--
THUK

WH-- WHAT?
SPLUT

COULDN'T YOU HAVE BEEN THAT QUICK EARLIER?!
I DIDN'T EVEN SEE HER THERE!

I'M ABOUT TO BE THE LAST THING YOU SEE--

VAMPIRELLA IS OUR FRIEND.
CARAWAY, NO!
I CAN'T BELIEVE YOU WERE GOING TO CUT MY HEAD OFF.
AND LEAVE THIS BODY?

AT LEAST SAVE THE REST OF ME FOR TAXIDERMY; THESE LEGS OUGHTA BE IN A MUSEUM.

AH, I CAN'T JUDGE Y'ALL BY THE COMP'NY YOU KEEP.
I ONCE SPENT THE BETTER PART OF A SUMMER UP IN THE BAY OF FUNDY, HUNTIN' THEIR LOCAL WATER BEAST WITH A BUNCHA NOVA SCOTIAN WERE-NARWHALS.
YEAH?
HOW ABOUT WE GET THE FUCK OUT OF DODGE, LEAVE ANY STILL-WRIGGLING VAMPIRES TRAPPED IN YOUR GARLIC PERIMETER 'TIL THE SUN COMES UP AND POPS THEIR HEADS, AND YOU TELL US ALL ABOUT THAT?

THROW IN A COUPLE'A CAMPFIRE DOGS, AND YOU GOT YOURSELF AN EVENING.

OH, HEY THERE.
SORRY, I'VE BEEN KIND OF QUIET UP HERE IN MY HEAD.
I GUESS WHEN I HAVE PEOPLE AROUND, FRIENDS OR WHATEVER, I DON'T HAVE TO CONSISTENTLY AMUSE MYSELF.
I CAN TAKE TURNS, DO THINGS FOR OTHER PEOPLE AND, I GUESS, LET THEM DO THINGS FOR ME.
--SO I WAS LIKE, "A SHOTGUN? I'M NOT REALLY A FAN," AND SHE PULLS OUT A JOINT.
AND WITH YOUR BOSS'S DAUGHTER, GIRL, YOU'RE A MESS.
YEAH, BUT THAT'S JUST ME.
SO WILL HAVERHILL RETURN TO NORMAL AFTER THIS?
HONESTLY?
I DON'T THINK I CARE.
MAYBE I GOTTA FIND SOMETHING NEW RATHER THAN ENDLESS REMAKES AND RESURRECTIONS OF PARTS OF MY LIFE BEFORE?
OR NOT.
OR NOT!
YEAH, YEAH...
OR NOT.
The End

ISSUE 12 COVER BY
TIM SEELEY & NICK FILARDI

ALTERNATE COVER BY
DANIEL LEISTER

TEAR OUT MY HEAAART, AND THROW IT ON THE FLOOOOOR AND I'M SORRY FOOOR GETTING BLOOD ON YOUR FLOOR
I'M NEVER LETTING YOU PICK THE MUSIC AGAIN.
IF YOU CAN'T TELL FROM VLAD'S MOOD MUSIC, THIS IS A VERY SPECIAL EPISODE.

MY HEART, CASSIE.
SHE IS BROKEN.
THAT'S YOUR BRAIN THAT'S BROKEN, VLAD, OLD BUDDY.
AND I THOUGHT YOU AND VAMPIRELLA ENDED THINGS MUTUALLY?

DESPITE OUR INTENSE PHYSICAL CHEMISTRY--
GROSS!
--WE ACCEPTED THAT WE DO NOT LEAD COMPATIBLE LIFESTYLES.
HOW BORING OF YOU.

OH, I SHOULD TAKE CASSIE'S ADVICE FOR GIRLFRIENDS, YES.
SHOULD I HAVE KILLED HER MOM, CASSIE?

DON'T WORRY; IT'S NOT A SPECIAL EPISODE ABOUT WHAT HAPPENS WHEN YOU MURDER YOUR BEST FRIEND.
WHAT THE @#$% DID YOU JUST SAY TO ME?!
SKREEE

THOUGH AFTER THAT, IT SHOULD BE.
THUNK KA CHUNK

TUCK AND ROLL, BUDDY, *TUCK AND ROLL!*
meep!

HNNNNGHHH!!
HNNNNGHHH!!
hnnnnghhh!!

OH GOD, WE'RE GONNA DIE!
FWAM

I'M SO READY!
TUMP

SQUEEEAK

DAMMIT! I GUESS WE LIVED.
UGGHHHHH...

VLAD!
OH @#$%, YOU OKAY?

WHAT DID YOU JUST SAY?
I ASKED IF YOU WERE OKAY, YOU BIG PALOOKA.

NO, BEFORE THAT.
UHHH...
HOLY @#$%--

OKAY, THAT WAS WEIRD.
DID YOU HEAR A BUNCH OF GARBLED PUNCTUATION TOO?
YES.
I HAVE NO IDEA HOW ONE WOULD PRONOUNCE THAT, BUT WHEN YOU SAID IT I FOUND IT IMMEDIATELY CLEAR.
WEIRD.

WELCOME TO
WERTHAM
"A Good Clean Place to Live!"
MAYOR
RICHARD WEINER
I HOPE THIS TOWN HAS FOOD.
I'M @#$%ING STARVING.
THERE IS THAT SOUND AGAIN.
I'M HECKA STARVING.
VERY STARVING.

THIS CITY IS MINE.

MINE TO PROTECT.
MINE TO RULE.

AND IF SOMEONE NEEDS TO PROTECT ITS PEOPLE FROM THEMSELVES...
LANNND
FINN

OH NO, NOT YOU!
I'M JUST READING IT FOR A COLLEGE ESSAY!
...I WILL...

CENSORED
AAAAAUGH!

...BY ANY MEANS NECESSARY.

JOEY'S
DINGALING
HELLO?

HEY, OUR TRUCK BROKE DOWN AND--

CAN I GET YOU A JACKET, OR PERHAPS A PONCHO?

ARE YOU KIDDING ME?
WE WALKED HERE FOR LIKE TWO MILES IN THE HEAT!
I THINK THE LITTLE PLACE WHERE MY THIGHS RUB TOGETHER IS BLEEDING.
PUT THAT AWAY!

I WILL NOT HAVE YOU MAKE THIS PLACE UNCLEAN!

DEPRESS

AUUUUUGH!
AUUUUUGH!
SHE DIDN'T EVEN ASK ABOUT THE TRUCK!
THEIR CUSTOMER SERVICE $@#%S!
THERE IS THAT SOUND AGAIN!
THIS!

WHOOSH
THIS!
NOT APPROVED BY THE COMICS CODE AUTHORITY

WHUMP
THIS!
OH.
VISITORS TO MY OFFICE.

HOW NICE.
NO. NOT NICE.
Dick Weiner

YOU WANNA EXPLAIN TO ME WHAT THE $#!+ IS GOING ON AND WHY WE JUST GOT DUMPED IN HERE OFF SOME SLIDE FROM DOUBLE DARE?!

YOUNG'UN, HERE IN WERTHAM WE DON'T SWEAR.
AND WE CERTAINLY DON'T WATCH DOUBLE DARE.

TAKE YOUR HAND OFF OF CASSIE'S FACE, OR I SWEAR I'LL CUT OFF YOUR--

WEINER?!
YOUR NAME IS LITERALLY DICK WEINER?!
HEH HEH HEH...
Dick Weiner

HEY NOW, LITTLE LADY, WHY DON'T YOU JUST PUT THAT DOWN IMMEDIATELY.
OKAY, OKAY. I'M CASSIE, THAT'S VLAD. NEITHER OF US ARE NAMED DICK-- UNFORTUNATELY.
WANT TO TELL US WHY WE GOT SECRET-SLIDED TO THE MAYOR'S UNDERGROUND JIGSAW-BASEMENT OFFICE BY THE OLD LADY AT THE MECHANICS SHOP, DICK?
OH, WHY YES.
YES, I MOST CERTAINLY DO.

THIS IS THE WERTHAM I GREW UP IN. PRETTIER'N A PEACH, AIN'T SHE?
AND THIS IS THE TOWN OF WERTHAM THAT PEOPLE DESERVE.
AS MAYOR, IT'S MY JOB TO ENSURE SHE STAYS CLEAN, HAPPY, AND UNSPOILT BY LIL NASTIES SUCH AS VIOLENCE, SWEARIN', AND DEVIANT SEX-SHOO-ALITY.
OHHHH. UH.
SO HOW COME WE CAN'T HEAR OURSELVES WHEN WE SAY "@@@@" AND "&&&&" AND "#$$@ MY GAPING %%%%%%% YOU #### JUGGLING THUNDER-$$$$"?

AH, THAT.
YOU THERE, BIG GUY.
??
YOU LOOK LIKE A MAN WHO HAS LIVED LIFE OFF OF THE BEATEN PATH.
Y'ALL UNDERSTAND THAT THERE ARE MAGICS IN THIS WORLD BEYOND THE UNDERSTANDING OF MOSTA THESE PEOPLE?

YES, UM. BUT WE ARE STILL JUST NEEDING OUR TRUCK FIXED?
AND I'D LIKE AN ANSWER ABOUT THE TRAP DOOR SLIDE, STILL.

OH, THAT'S JUST SOMETHING I HAD PUT TOGETHER SO I COULD MAKE SURE I KEEP AN EYE ON ALL THE NEW VISITORS WHO COME TO TOWN!
NOTHIN' LIKE A COMPLEX NETWORK OF UNDERGROUND TUBES TO MONITOR DEVIANT BEHAVIORS, Y'ALL!

WE'LL GET THAT TRUCK'A YOURS FIXED UP IN A JIFFY OF A LUBE, TRUST.

WHAT THE--
--HECK-A-ROONIE--
--JUST HAPPENED?

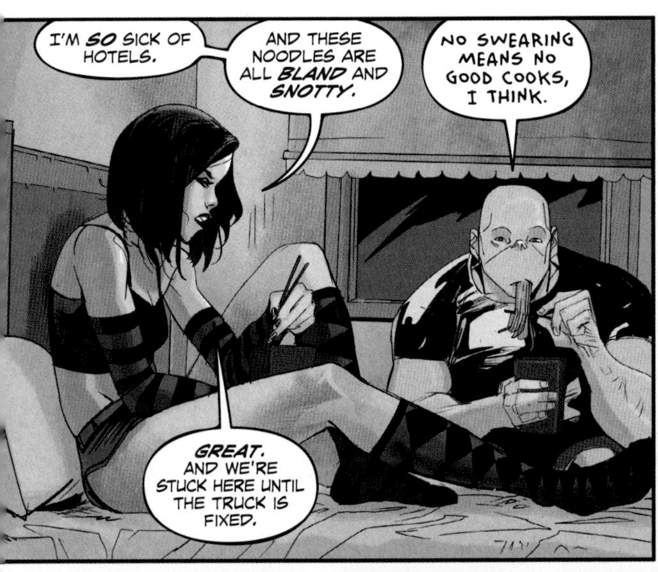
I'M SO SICK OF HOTELS.
AND THESE NOODLES ARE ALL BLAND AND SNOTTY.
NO SWEARING MEANS NO GOOD COOKS, I THINK.
GREAT. AND WE'RE STUCK HERE UNTIL THE TRUCK IS FIXED.

NOK NOK
MAYBE NOT?
OH?

I WONDER IF WHEN I BRAIN SOMEONE IN THIS TOWN, CANDY COMES OUT.

HEY.
YOU CALLED LAURIE?!

SLAM
CASSIE!

THAT RELATIONSHIP IS DEAD, AND YOU KNOW WHAT I DO TO THINGS THAT COME BACK FROM THE DEAD, BUDDY?
I CALLED HER, CASSIE.

WHY WOULD YOU DO THAT?
BECAUSE WE ARE IN A BAD SITUATION, I THINK.
I DO NOT TRUST THIS MAYOR, NOR DO I TRUST HIS NO-SWEARING-MAGICS, HIS DOUBLE DARE SLIDE, OR HIS OFFICE WITH A DRAIN IN THE FLOOR.
WE NEED HELP.
flrrr

I AM SORRY LAURIE. PLEASE COME INTO THE ROOM.
WANT SOME NOODLES?
THEY'RE *TERRIBLE*.
HEY THERE. NO THANKS.

HOW ARE YOU, LAURIE, SINCE WE LAS SPOKE
I'M SORRY I KILLED YOUR MOM--
LISTE ABOUT MY MOM...
YOU FIRST.
mrrowrpftt!

MY MOTHER WAS A COMPLICATED PERSON. SO ARE YOU.
BUT I'VE COME TO REALIZE THE DIFFERENCE BETWEEN THE TWO OF YOU IS THAT YOU WANT TO DO GOOD, IN YOUR OWN STUPID, BLOODY, VIOLENT WAY, AND SHE WANTED TO ACTIVELY DO *EVIL*.

SO WE'RE--
CASSIE, YOU WERE REALLY IMPORTANT TO ME AT A TIME IN MY LIFE, AND VLAD SOUNDED SCARED ON THE PHONE.
IF YOU WANT TO KNOW WHAT I AM TO YOU NOW, IT'S A *LIFELINE* OUT OF HERE, AND THAT'S IT, OKAY?

CAN YOU GIVE US A RIDE OUT OF HERE?
I CAN'T, ACTUALLY.
THE ONLY WAY I COULD GET HERE ON SHORT NOTICE WAS TO TAKE THE *BIKE*.
I'M SORRY.

COOL, STRANDED IN A TOWN RUN BY MAYOR DICK JIGSAW, AND MY EX SHOWS UP JUST TO LET ME DOWN.
WAS I, LIKE, A PUPPY-DROWNER IN A PAST LIFE?
CASSIE IS MEANING TO SAY, "THANK YOU, LAURIE."

I SEE THAT.
IF NOTHING ELSE, I'M ANOTHER WARM BODY TO FIGHT YOUR WAY OUT OF HERE.

JUST WHEN I FORGET THAT YOU'RE MY TYPE OF GIRL...

"...YOU GO AND REMIND ME."
SO WHAT IS YOUR PLAN?
LEAVE DARIO IN THE HOTEL ROOM AND PROVOKE THIS @#$-CLOWN INTO SHOWING UP.
I GUESS I DON'T BELIEVE THAT IN A PLACE WITH TRAP DOORS, BLEEPING IS ALL THEY DO TO PEOPLE WHO SWEAR AND MAKE A FUSS.
WELL, YOU READY?
@#$% YEAH.
HWUFFFFF

HEY ****STICK! BRING YOUR WRINKLED $%^HOLE OUT HERE AND FIGHT MY HALF-NAKED &&& BEFORE I HUNT YOU DOWN LIKE A BLOODHOUND AND MAKE TAPENADE OUT OF YOUR GUTTY-WORKS!
I'M NOT PLAYING WITH YOU, YOU ^%$#-FILLED @#$%-FOR-BRAINS SAD SACK OF *^%$!
SHOW UP AND GET BENT!
HEY, CASSIE?
YEAH, WHAT?
HMPH--!
THIS IS NOT SIMPLY MY LONELINESS TALKING, BUT I DO NOT THINK IT IS A GOOD TIME--

UM, SO--
DON'T GET TOO EXCITED.
RUMMMMMBLE
WHO THE #$%! ARE YOU?
NO ONE KNOWS WHAT DRIVES THIS DARK FIGURE TO HIS WORK, LIMITING SEX, VIOLENCE, AND CRITICAL THOUGHT ALL OVER WERTHAM. IN THE DARK OF THE NIGHT, HE APPEARS, TO LAY HIS MIGHTY STAMP TO THE FACES OF THOSE WHO WOULD SEEK TO CHECK OUT GROWN-UP BOOKS FROM THE LOCAL LIBRARY. HE IS--
--THE CENSOR.
KRAKOW
GET OFF OF ONE ANOTHER.
I'D RATHER US GET OFF ON ONE ANOTHER.
BUT YOU SEEM TO HAVE SOME SORT OF PROBLEM WITH THAT?
HUP!

UM, ER--
HEY!

NOOO!

YOU'RE NOT SUPPOSED TO DO THAT HERE!

BUT GESTURES ARE--HNGKK--NOTORIOUSLY--HRG--HARD TO CENSOR!
LAURIE!
HIT HIM!

WHAT THE--?!
THUK
BLOOD IS RATED M, GIRL.
WE DON'T HAVE THAT HERE.
OH YEAH?
YOU CAN CENSOR ALL THE BLOOD YOU LIKE, BUT AFTER EATING THOSE CRAPPY NOODLES, I'M PRETTY SURE SOMETHING'LL COME OUT IF YOU HIT ME IN THE GUT!
UNCLEAN!
OH DUDE, I'M FILTHY.
FLUMP
THAT'S M-RATED, TOO.

SO IT HAD TO GO.
AW, YUCK!
I DON'T LIKE DICK PICS AT THE *BEST* OF TIMES--
--AND I LIKE THEM EVEN LESS WHEN IT LOOKS LIKE IT WAS SEDUCED BY A WEED WHACKER.

CASSIE, HIT HIM!

TOO SLOW!
HUP--

OOOF!
TOO SLOW.
LAURIE!

YOUR *MIND* IS *CLOUDED* WITH *LUST* AND *INDECENCY.*
I WILL SET YOU FREE.

HE IS GOING TO KILL LAURIE!
WE HAVE TO DISTRACT HIM, HE'S CREEPILY SINGLE-MINDED.
THIS IS THE ONLY THING HE CARES ABOUT!

MMMMMMWAH! MWAH--
STOP. CASSIE, STOP IT!

YOU KNOW I DON'T LIKE THAT ANY MORE THAN YOU DO, BUT IF HE WANTS INDECENCY TO PUNISH--
IT ISN'T WORKING, CASSIE.

HE ONLY SEEMED TO THINK IT WAS INDECENT WHEN IT WAS YOU AND LAURIE KISSING.
OH.

ONLY WHEN IT WAS--
I SEE.

WHAT'S GOING ON?
VLAD, WOULD YOU EXCUSE ME FOR A MOMENT?
I HEARD A FIGHT!

HALT! HANDS WHERE WE CAN SEE 'EM!

HEY, WHAT'S THE DEAL?
THE CENSOR'S BEEN PATROLLING THESE STREETS FOR SOME TIME.
BUT ATTACKING VISITORS IN THE STREET IS A STEP TOO FAR. WE'VE NEVER BEEN ABLE TO UNCOVER HIS TRUE IDENTITY.

DID YOU EVER THINK TO LOOK INTO THE GUY WHO BUILT A NETWORK OF FLOOR-DRAIN BASEMENTS UNDER THE ENTIRE TOWN?
OH, WOW. ACTUALLY.
HEY BURT, WE SHOULD PROBABLY LOOK INTO THAT.

IT'S ALMOST LIKE SEVERELY LIMITING ACCESS TO BOOKS AND OTHER MEDIA REALLY DAMPENS THE DEVELOPMENT OF ONE'S CRITICAL THINKING SKILLS!
WHO WOULD HAVE THUNK?

NOW LET'S SEE WHO THIS JOKER IS--

MAYOR DICK WEINER?!
WELL, LIKE, OBVIOUSLY.
WHO THE HELL ELSE WOULD IT HAVE BEEN?

Y'ALL DON'T UNDERSTAND! WHEN I WAS BORN MY MAMA CALLED ME DICK WEINER! I NEVER HAD A CHANCE!
Y'ALL'S MERCILESS CRUELTY FILLED ME WITH SUCH A RAGE!

WE'VE GOT THIS ONE, BOYS.
YOUR SMALL-TOWN MAYOR ISN'T A HUMAN, HE'S A SLASHER.
HE PROBABLY DIED LONG AGO WITH A SADNESS OR ANGER DEEP IN HIS HEART, ONLY TO RETURN TO LIFE AND PUNISH HAPPY CAMPERS.
THE PRIEST MADE A DICK JOKE DURIN' MY EULOGY!

LEGALLY HE'S BEEN DEAD SINCE 1989, SO YOU CAN JUST HAND HIM OVER TO US FOR DISPOSAL.
LAURIE DID THE RESEARCH.

NOW LET'S GET OUR TRUCK FIXED AND BLOW THIS HELLHOLE.
THE END!
WAIT.
NAH.

HOW'S THE WOOD CHOPPING GOING, BUDDY?
EASIER NOW THAT I CAN SWEAR.
AND IT HELPS MY SADNESS ABOUT VAMPIRELLA.
SHE WOULD HAVE LOVED TO SCARE THE LOCALS IN A PLACE LIKE THIS.
AWW, BUDDY.
WOULD YOU LIKE TO DO THE HONOR OF DISPOSING OF DICK WEINER'S CORPSE?
READY?
THREE... TWO...
WHRRR
KASHLUNK
lum!
FUCK YEAH.
~fin~

HACK/SLASH RESURRECTION
GALLERY

SKETCH BY TIM SEELEY

PIN-UP BY CELOR & K. MICHAEL RUSSELL

ALTERNATE COVER BY TIM SEELEY

SKETCHES BY TIM SEELEY

From the pages of HACK/SLASH!

image

Cat & Dog

INVESTIGATIONS

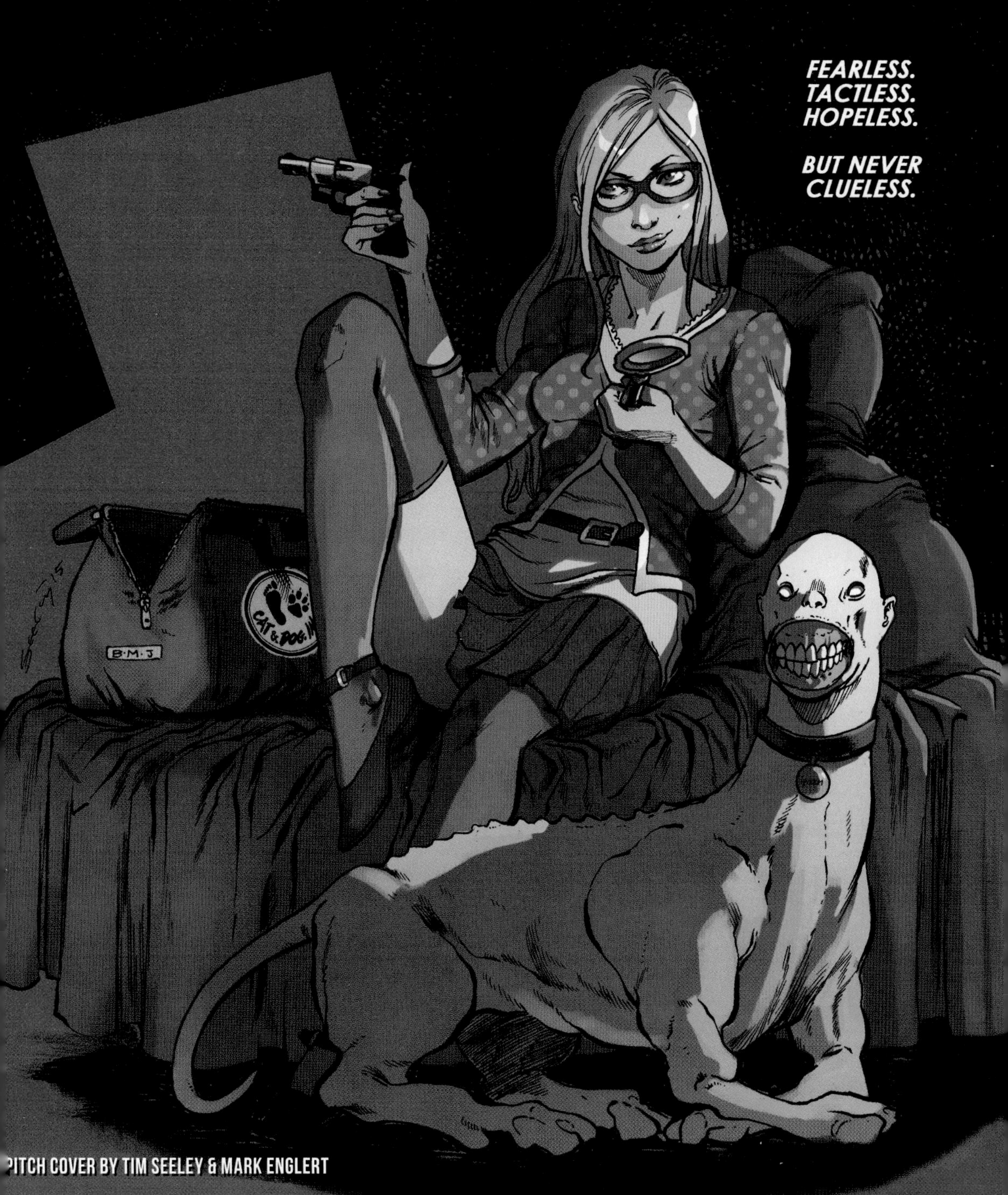

PITCH COVER BY TIM SEELEY & MARK ENGLERT

PITCH COVER BY JOHN ZYLSTRA

CAT CURIO & POOCH REDESIGN BY TIM SEELEY

ALTERNATE COVER COVER BY TIM SEELEY & ADDISON DUKE

PIN-UP BY TIM SEELEY

PIN-UP BY TIM SEELEY